Sunbather

This story is placed under my authorship, though technically I did not write the following words and was merely the person who found them.

On the thirteenth of August my girlfriend and I went for a day trip to Creswell Crags, a limestone gorge on the edge of Nottinghamshire that is home to a multitude of accessible caves that once housed primitive humans some 10,000 years ago. We'd decided to visit as a recent discovery of apotropaic marks, ancient markings used to "turn away" evil, was being showcased to the public. When we arrived, we noticed a car parked on a strange angle, somewhat hidden by overgrowth with smashed windows. Catherine didn't want to inspect it further and a part of me wishes that I had listened. The car itself was completely empty, except for the notebook placed on the front passenger seat. Catherine wanted to leave it there but I've always been super curious and I hoped to unearth some great mystery, like in a video game or adventure film, so I took it. I have edited where appropriate but have not changed the essence of the story. The details within are as they were written in the notebook when it was found; I've merely added a little artistic flair to pad out what was essentially scribbled shorthand to make it a flowing narrative.

The title Sunbather was written on the first page of the notebook. The only thing I can find a connection with is that Sunbather is the title of an album by an American Black Metal band named Deafheaven, and this story begins at a Black Metal concert. I have reached out to the band and they kindly replied, assuring me that the details of the notebook I found had nothing to do with them or their music.

There's that stupid cliché of curiosity killed the cat, or be careful what you wish for, but the obsession I've had with this notebook has become a huge detriment to my life. It has almost destroyed my social life, my work and my relationship. This is why I'm finally releasing this story; I can't just let it go but I can't keep tumbling down this rabbit hole alone. I'm hoping that by putting it out there someone will be able to solve what I have yet been unable to.

Frank Floyd.

"This is the day that God died."

They looked at each other, a telekinetic game of Chinese Whispers, as if the information that was about to proceed that statement was being transferred silently through the air like an invisible frequency only they could tune into. This inaudible transmission was seemingly acknowledged with the slight nods exchanged between all four of the people sat in front of me. Until one of them opened their mouths to release the air vibrations of their collective thoughts, all I could do was merely wait in anticipation.

"Aceasta este ziua in care Dumnezeu a murit....it means this is the day that God died."

Another bout of silence. This one however, was orchestrated from my side of the battlefield. It was an old trick to get them to relinquish additional information. Leaving the silence hanging in the air would kill them, the awkwardness too much for any person to bare. I loved the silence; this moment before more words flooded out, I bathed in it. I could dive into an ocean of this noiseless tension and keep swimming down into its depths until time itself ended. Until there was nothing left but a vacuous lingering from an existence that once was and never would be again. Sometimes the air would be broken from the unearthing of some golden nugget of intellect that shed far more light onto the mystery than had been previously illuminated. Sometimes what tumbled out was an empty and hollow cacophony of words merely for the purpose of filling the vast void I'd left for them to drown in. Either way, the silence was always broken by my opposition and never by myself. I concealed my victory smirk as I saw one of the four suck air through their nostrils in preparation for the words that would follow.

"We thought it sounded cool."

A lacklustre response, hardly worth the wait that preceded it, though the foursome across from me seemed satisfied with the outcome. They'd successfully traversed across a minefield of my planting and come out the other side unscathed. Though I hated to admit it, they now had me at checkmate. This was the end and all I could do was move on and deal with the wake from this segment of our mutual interaction.

I glanced momentarily at the Dictaphone on the table. The LCD display danced up and down with a combination of green, yellow and red, all indicating that the small device was keeping a permanent record of the conversation. I glanced back and the four of them were staring like hungry wolves at the door of my next question.

"How does it feel to finally be playing to your fans here in the U.K.?"

The band's name was Crimsona. A Romanian Ambient Black Metal outfit who had recently released their debut album, Aceasta Este Ziua in Care Dumnezeu a Murit. The group had a solid fan base in the U.K. metal scene thanks to their single Sete De Sânge, roughly translated to Bloodlust, being the title track in a recent horror film that smashed box office figures across the country. I'd reviewed the album for Louder Than War, an online alternative music magazine, and the band had liked the review so much they contacted me personally to request an interview when they hit the shores of merry old England to play their first shows over here. My writing wasn't paid, but it was a good way to keep myself occupied. The Devil finds work for idle hands and all that, plus I got free entry to most shows.

I knew my stuff when it came to Black Metal. Back when I was in college, I'd read a book about its origins in Norway; a bloody few years during the nineties filled with betrayal, occult ritual, and even murder of fellow musicians in a race to become the most evil member within the scene. This brutality had dispersed across most of the northern hemisphere, with Black Metal enthusiasts in the U.K., U.S.A., Finland, and many Eastern European countries. Its initial surge eventually died out, leaving only a few remaining faithful adherents to the genre. I'd read up on Anton LaVey and found his work surprisingly benevolent and often very poignant, but when the surface of Satanism was scratched there was a much darker underbelly. A whole sinister subculture of devotees for the Devil who, unlike LaVey, took the worship of Satan all too literal. The further I dove into that vast rabbit-hole the weirder it got. Some members of the scene had moved on from Satan worship and now prayed to the old Norse gods. Others had nose-dived into the infinite stream of conspiracy theories believing the earth was hollow, with Hitler clones being kept in the centre waiting for the right time to strike and create a Fourth Reich. Some of the few members still loyal to Lucifer had even attempted to summon the antichrist to bring forth an age of hell on earth. Thankfully the four across from me seemed very much in the less extreme camps, one of them even donning a t-shirt with the bald-headed grimace of LaVey staring menacingly with a snake wrapped around his shoulders. As they drank their beers and laughed through our interview, I felt very much in good company and gradually allowed myself to relax as if I was spending time with close friends.

This show in Manchester was the first of only a handful of dates across the U.K. that would keep the four tied to the island for the next two weeks. Although the band had gained notoriety from their Hollywood horror hit, their following was solely from within the metal scene and in recent years the numbers of loyal gig-goers had dwindled. The vast subculture of live heavy metal was a dying beast, with only the most die-hard keeping its heart beating. Still, the band seemed satisfied that the eight hundred capacity venue tonight would be filled to its maximum so they could create an amazing show and make their near two-thousand-mile journey worth it.

I knew the owner of the venue well. He'd moved to England a few years back from Romania and set up the venue. The band playing tonight were close friends of his from back home. When he shook my hand for the first time he gripped it a little too hard, and a weather warning worthy amount of spit had flown from his mouth to crash into the white cliffs of my cheeks when he told me his name.

"Eytan."

I was never sure if that was his first name or just a nickname, and I never asked, but as he hit the plosive "T" which began the second syllable of his moniker, that was when the torrents of saliva graced my face. I knew it was rude to draw attention to this, so I waited the full ten minutes of our initial conversation with the feeling of his spit being pulled by the weight of gravity down through the surface of my skin before I wiped it away.

I'd been introduced to him one night by the singer of a local band called Ten Foot Wizard. I'd interviewed them before one of their shows and then offered to help sell their merchandise while they played. The owner had chipped in too, and we spoke most the night whilst selling a modest number of CDs and tees. The shirts were adorned with an old man with a giant beard, whose facial tendrils went on to form the name of the band. The design was so impressive that I wanted one for myself. I tried to pay but the band refused and called it "not a gift but payment for my help". The owner slapped my back hard and said, "You ever want some odd jobs then come to me!" When I told him I already had enough t-shirts he guffawed into the air in an almost parodic way before straightening his face into a stony stare; the polar opposite of the animation that had preceded it. "I'll pay you with money, of course." At first I thought he was joking but at the end of the night he took my number and said he'd be in touch soon. He phoned a few days later asking for some help with the new paint job he'd planned for the bathrooms. God knows why he bothered; we painted them a light grey and they were covered with graffiti again a few weeks after. I was paid a lot more than I had expected and was assured I'd be roped in for more work as and when it was needed. He phoned again the next day and the day after that, there were always jobs and I was always available. This is how I became a regular face of the Rebellion Bar.

We finished up the interview and the band headed to the bar to order more drinks. This would be their fifth round and it had only just passed three in the afternoon. The time of day clearly didn't matter to them, but it mattered even less to me. I switched off the Dictaphone and wrote some last-minute scribbles in my notebook to aid with the write-up the next day. In the past I'd had some solid ideas and not jotted them down quick enough, forgetting the content of their existence before it was time to put word to page. After making this mistake one too many times, I'd decided to constantly carry a small notepad with me. The one currently being filled was given to me by Eytan. He told me he found it in the venue whilst cleaning one night and that he thought I'd find a much better use for it. I snapped the red elastic strap over the black faux-leather front just as the man who had gifted me the notebook headed over.

"Wanna get paid?"

"What's the job?" I replied.

I spent the evening on the door, in no way any form of authority, simply tasked with checking tickets. I would draw a large black X on back of the hands of anyone who came in and turned away those who hadn't managed to get tickets before it had sold out. I was in a perfect vantage point where

I could see the stage whilst also keeping an eye on the entrance. There were two acts that evening, the opener being a Doom Metal band named Bong Cauldron. The drone of slow, heavy, bass riffs thundered over a crowd of slowly increasing magnitude until, by the end of their first song, the entire building was near to capacity. It was when their set began to come closer to its end, as the first blast of distortion from their penultimate song flooded out across the room, that she walked over, seemingly tipsy but still in full control of her motor functions. She leaned right across into my face in order to be heard over the noise and with the strong smell of vodka closely following her words, screamed,

"I want to purchase Bong Cauldron music!"

Her voice had a strong East-European accent, not as heavy as that of the band I had spoken to hours ago, with just enough of it lost to imply that a long time had elapsed since she'd last been in her home country. It was as if the subtle edges of another accent had invaded her throat and waged a protracted war of integration, the native tongue fighting strong but slowly losing. I explained that I wasn't actually anything to do with the band and that I was merely on the doors, that perhaps she'd like to come back in a few minutes when they'd finished their set. She pointed longingly at the stack of CDs less than a metre away from me, before realising the exact meaning of my words and moving back from her inches away proximity. Her expression changed from excited curiosity into one of complete defeat. She stood there with silent rumination, mulling on her next course of action. She was short, and though a slight distance had been put between us now I could tell she wasn't much taller than my shoulders. Her hair was almost entirely pitch-black except for one pure white streak that only appeared when she shook her head, which she did as if in defiance of my refusal to assist. When that streak flitted out it looked as if a bolt of lightning was tearing across the twilight of her long, dark locks. I noticed, moving with the swing of her head, a necklace with a small sapphire stone as its pendant. Her eyes were a deep, emerald green and were encased with heavy circles of black eye shadow that covered the entire orbit. I apologised for not being able to help her and tried to mirror her expression of woe in order to give off some kind of sincere empathy. She smiled, reassuring me that her pain was only fleeting.

"You have sadness in your eyes. It is only CD. I can buy later."

Before I could respond, her cheeks filled up like a cartoon hamster and her eyes widened with an equal dose of unexpected shock, making the dark eye shadow retreat from the daylight of her pale white sclera. She waved her hand at me, perhaps as a goodbye or some other way of excusing herself, before running back into the crowd and disappearing from sight to presumably vomit in the bathrooms.

The music of the evening closed with a heavy scent of sweat and adrenaline lingering in the air. Crimsona finished their final song, letting the final chord drone out into the crowd before the quartet bellowed in unison "AVE SATANAS" with raised fists. The crowd mirrored this salute, willing participants in the ritualistic dogma of the entire show. There had been a constant littering of occult-inspired symbolism throughout the band's set in the form of vocal calls-to-arm from the members, as well as the macabre mise-en-scene surrounding the four. Faux-severed pig heads on pikes, a limbless prosthetic human corpse as decoration for one of the mic stands, and a large black backdrop that was emblazoned with a deep red symbol that I recognised but couldn't name. The strangest part of the entire show was midway through, when Crimsona discarded their instruments and traded them for black robes. They knelt centre stage, facing each other and seemingly ignorant of the crowd, and began chanting in hushed tones that would have only been audible if amplified by one of the microphones that had been moved aside. I tried to hear these words, with not the slightest shred of success, failing to pick up even a single bit of what was being said by the four huddled figures. They then removed their robes and returned to playing, the crowd perplexed but slowly falling back into the atmosphere of the music.

The crowd flooded out, a sea of darkened clothing and smeared corpse-paint, and soon the venue was empty. The band had packed up their gear, leaving it piled neatly on the stage, and headed to their hotel with the promise to return for their equipment tomorrow. Eytan appeared from a door that was marked STAFF ONLY. Although I wasn't officially staff it felt strange realising that I had no idea what was behind there, that I'd been doing odd jobs for some time, but I'd never seen the entire building. He asked me to do one last sweep of the venue as he handed a small clear plastic bag filled with the payment for my work. The bar was pretty open, so it was easy to do a spot check and make sure no one was left within its walls. As I checked the female toilets, I found in an unlocked stall the girl with the jet-black hair. She was unconscious, sat on the toilet with her jeans and knickers around her ankles, her head against the stall wall with her mouth agape and a slight sliver of drool dangling from her lip. Even though the only

17

person within earshot was passed out and unable to respond I still felt the need to make audible my reaction to this scene.

"Shit."

I left her there while I went to track down Eytan and inform him of the drunken girl completely out of it in the female bathroom. We carved out a plan of action, returning to the stall, redressing her with careful attention to maintain as much of her dignity as possible, before carrying her by ankles and shoulders back into the main hall and placing her on the large beat up sofa at the back.

"I'll stay here and keep an eye on her. Make sure there's someone there to explain when she wakes up."

Eytan simply nodded in agreement. He locked the main door and hung the key behind the bar before walking back through the door marked STAFF ONLY and into whatever mystery was held behind.

I moved the girl into the foetal position, she was laying on her back and thoughts of her choking on vomit in the night plagued my mind, before unzipping my jacket and placing it over her like a blanket. She stirred momentarily when I draped it over, wriggling her nose and shuffling slightly. I pulled two single seat sofas together, creating a makeshift bed for myself. I rolled over the arms and into the cocoon I had created. The girl with the raven hair snored, but it was so subtle it was almost like the humming of a song. I listened to the melody of her slumber and soon drifted off to its lullaby.

When I woke in the morning the girl was already awake. She was sat upright, alert and with no sign of the catastrophic state she was in the night before. Staring directly at me and smiling a wide grin she asked,

"You took care of me?"

I explained what had happened, how we'd spoke before she had vanished into the crowd only to find her passed out, and she nodded as the light of those memories seeped through the dark cover of her drunken haze.

"I remember you. You had sad eyes."

She stood up and put on the jacket I'd draped over her, leaned in closer towards me and inspected my face with the intense look of a detective. I wiped the sleep away to cooperate with her investigation. She leaned back and smiled again, seemingly satisfied.

"They're still sad but seem a little happier today."

I stretched out and split the cocoon I'd been nesting in. Standing up my entire body ached from sleeping in such a cramped state. All the while the girl stood stoically, smiling.

"What is your name?"

I told her, and then asked her the same.

"Mara."

I'd told her my full name, and instantly regretted the formality of doing so when she replied with just her first. "So, Sheldon Belmond, what are we to do today? I must repay you for being my hero."

She said my name with the Eastern-European accent coming through stronger than it had with other words. Sheldon became "Cheldon" and Belmond sounded more like she was saying "Bailmond."

21

I searched the room by rotating a full three hundred and sixty degrees on the spot. With no sign of Eytan, I took the key from behind the bar and released us both into the retina scorching light of the day. Mara flicked the hood of my jacket over head to shield her from the sun, while I locked the door again from the outside and posted the key through the letterbox.

We went into the first café we passed. I ordered a black coffee and Mara asked for an espresso with pouring cream on the side. She mentioned something in passing about how in Romania they drank something in the coffee called kaymak, which was essentially cream anyway. I tried to pay for the drinks, but she insisted that she owed me for taking care of her. We sat outside, the morning sun high and beaming on the front of the coffee shop.

"So, you're from Romania?" I asked.

She poured the cream into her cup and stirred purposefully. The juxtaposing shades were initially starkly contrasted but as the tempest she had created swirled the two liquids, they merged until darkness and light were one and the same.

"Yes. It is why I was at the show last night. I like the band because they remind me of home."

Mara told me she had been in England for just over a year, studying at university. When I asked what she was studying, the word Psychology was followed by what felt like an infinite pause as she mulled over her next words, her eyes rolling in up into the lids as if the next sentence was hidden behind them.

"I am interested in death. How people react to death. The stages of grief and how it affects people.

Everyone reacts very differently. Some cases are very bad. People erase the memory, they don't remember it happened at all, or they create…. what is the word? Illusion? Yes, their brain creates an illusion. Or if it's really bad, sometimes the people go crazy."

The words she spoke caused a gust of air to stall within my lungs. My heart swelled and my head filled with adrenaline. I felt the physical sensations of anxiety cascade over my entire being and I slowly closed my eyes to try and stop the world from spinning. The words had been a punch to the gut and the lingering awkwardness of my inability to respond was the dizzying feeling after the blow.

"Oh."

"You think is weird?"

The Romanian accent once again appearing strong as she incorrectly asked the question, completely omitting the existence of the word "it" as if it had no right to ever be placed within the structure of her query.

"It isn't that. It sounds interesting."

I sipped at the coffee and pleaded internally that this moment would end and the conversation would veer down an entirely different avenue, any direction that wasn't towards the topic of death or the grief that came thereafter. Thankfully she seemed to sense the atmosphere of this line of inquiry and steered it into another direction, blushing slightly.

"I was very drunk last night."

I placed the coffee down and let a small smile appear across my lips. She seemed ashamed, perhaps even vulnerable, as if the worry of judgement was a weight too much to bear. Though it was cruel, I decided to tease.

"You really were. I can't believe you vomited on that girl's shoes!"

Her mouth dropped open, her eyes bulging slightly in disbelief. I allowed the small smile slowly to stretch into a full-blown grin. She shook her head and the streak of lightning struck out again. We laughed a little too loud and the old couple on the table across from us shot short menacing glances as if laughter was some form of lewd behaviour to be condemned.

We sat outside that café for longer than I'd spent with another person in a very long time. We talked about everything and nothing, the lightning shooting out each time she shook her head. She'd occasionally scrunch up her nose, wriggling it like she did the night before while she slept, reminiscent of that old T.V. show about a young witch living in the mortal world. Mara would play with the sapphire stone around her neck each time she did so.

"I like your necklace."

Mara held the pendant of the necklace between two fingers when she replied.

"Thank you. It was a gift from my father. It sounds strange, but you remind me of him."

Mara told me about her studies and her love of heavy music, yet by the end of our stint sat outside in the sun, I still felt an incredible mystery surrounded her. She hadn't once mentioned what life had been like before she moved to England. She had spoken freely and openly with no indication of secrecy in her words on every other topic, but would answer any questions about her life in Romania with an abrupt bluntness, without a single iota of emotion or detail. I didn't know her beyond the small details given during this first conversation, yet I felt a strong connection to her. It felt the same way as meeting a girl during adolescence and thinking after even a short while that you knew this person would have a strong impact on your life, in some way at least. There was something incredibly alluring about Mara, an almost hypnotic quality that I couldn't put my finger on. Her speech was broken English, not bad but not quite fluent, and I was hooked on her every word. It was a feeling that I hadn't expected, like the shock of a wasp sting or the leaping of your heart when you trip off a kerb.

"I would like to see you again very much" she said eventually, looking towards her now near-empty cup whilst using her spoon to toy with the last few remnants within it. She avoided eye contact as if I was some sort of medusa, as if one stare before my answer would lock her into the brutal anticipation that undoubtedly led after such a question had been asked.

"I'd like that too."

She looked up for a split second and smiled, before holding her hand out. I pulled my phone from my pocket, unlocked it, and passed it over. Her fingers nimbly tapped at the display for a while before handing it back over.

Mara lived in the student area of Manchester, only a few minutes out of the direct centre, and insisted that she walk me to the bus stop. As we strolled in the sun, she slid her hand into mine with such nonchalance it was as if a mild breeze had merely blown her palm into mine. As our fingers interlaced a jolt of electric shot through my arm, up the back of my neck, and struck my brain causing an influx of emetic guilt that sparked the adrenal rush of a flight or fight response. It felt as if just allowing this moment was akin to some deeply devious and illicit affair, the kind that destroys marriages that have lasted through decades of hardships, finally giving weight to the unbearable turmoil with one of the members secretly searching out greener pastures. Why did it feel like that? Why did it feel like a betrayal? Logically, there were no grounds for such emotions. There was no deceit, no affair, no one waiting at home comforted in ignorance of the actions, unaware that the trust and love that had been built over the years was being stripped out by a pure and carnal lust. My home was empty. I should just enjoy the comfort of another person's touch. But I couldn't. I didn't release my grip, but simply drowned in these sorts of thoughts until we finally arrived at the bus stop.

It wasn't long until the bus rounded the corner and we said our goodbyes. I hugged her, placing my arms under hers. As I did, she climbed my spine with one hand until her fingers were deep within the tendrils of my hair. As we separated that hand fell from its station and graced my jawline. She looked into my eyes, we were mere inches away, before leaning in and attempting to kiss me. Her lips were left with nothing but the hot air of the day upon them as I backed away.

I didn't make eye contact. There was nothing that I could say that would comfort, but I had to say something. To simply turn and walk onto that bus without a word would have been a punishment that no human should inflict onto another. But I didn't know what to say. It was only a few seconds but the static in the air lingered for an eternity.

Finally, I inhaled.

"I'll call you. I promise."

I leaned towards Mara and kissed her forehead before boarding the bus. She stood smiling as I took my seat and the vehicle began to depart, an almost impenetrable game face placed to hide the rejection. As I looked from the window at Mara, the first girl to have shown genuine affection towards me in two years, and the first for me to show genuine affection to in return, all I could think about is how much I missed Emma.

II

"You left your notebook. Come pick up your shit or it's going in the bin."

It was seven in the morning when my phone let off a resounding ping. It woke me from my slumber as my hand automatically reached out to my phone with no need to open my eyes. My alarm was set for only half an hour later, so I decided to deal with the message and start my day a little earlier. Though the name was displayed at the top of the screen, I could have figured by the blunt rudeness of the wording that it was Eytan. I had also learned not to take anything he said to heart. Whether his abruptness was a personality trait, or due to some cultural difference, remained a mystery but I knew it was completely innocent as when in person the insult was always said with a smile.

I washed, dressed, ate, and then headed into Manchester, taking the bus with all the usual sardines packed in, with little air or elbow room, on their commute to work. Rebellion was locked with the curtains drawn, so I banged hard on the door hoping Eytan would hear the thunder from whatever dark recess of the venue he was hiding. A long time passed with no response, so I pulled my phone from my pocket and clicked his name from the contact list. The call didn't even have the time to connect before the door was being unlocked and a face peered through the ajar entryway. Eytan winced at the sight of the sun and kept the door as close to shut as possible, as if the daylight was a virus attempting to infect the comfort of the darkness within. He grunted in acknowledgement of my presence, his eyes barely more than slits fighting against the light. Eytan then headed into the venue for a few moments before tossing the notebook towards me and slamming the door closed. I heard the lock click and then silence. I knew that my current interaction with Eytan had now ended.

It was my notebook, yet something was off. The black faux-leather front and the red elastic strap were the same, but there was something additional on its front. I recognised the symbol, the same symbol I saw on the stage the last time I was at Rebellion, the symbol I recognised but could not place the name of. A double cross with an infinity type motif attached.

I knew it had something to do with the Devil, but no matter how hard I tried to excavate the mineshafts of my memory I couldn't dig up that golden nugget of information. Staring at the symbol, it was obvious it had been scratched into the cover in an aggressive manner. I stood at the doorstep for an eternity with the notebook in my hand entranced by the artwork now etched into its cover. The mystery of the entire thing split my mind in two. The logical part figured that the carving was simply innocent, someone had found the notebook and merely scratched the surface out of boredom or, at worst, as some kind of dumb prank to freak out whoever found it. My emotional reaction, however, felt a much more sinister force emanating from the occult symbol staring back at me. I knew that only by pulling back the red elastic strap and opening the pages could I find potential answers as to who had invaded and vandalised my private scribblings. The emotional overweighed the logical; instead of paying no heed to the conspiracies crawling across my neural network, instead of sliding the notebook into my back pocket and continuing with my day, I split the pad open right there on the doorstep of Rebellion. What I found within sent a wave of pure panic across my entire being. The hot sun of the day was thwarted by the shivers and shakings of a full-blown anxiety attack.

Each page I'd written on had now been erased by means of thick black crosses filling the entire page. Only a few words and white space remained. The hand that had placed the giant X across each page had done so erratically. The crosses were so large and aggressive that each page was almost a complete blackout. I stared in terror at the months of notes that were now lost within this mess of dark ink. About midway through the word genocide, white pages began to show again and after a few blank pages there was fresh writing. Although clearly written in a steadier pace, there was still that same chaos to the script as was in the crosses that had preceded.

As Views Expand.

StAre at The sun.

As Night Approaches.

S...

The final word was unfinished. It trailed off and was lost in page after page of empty white nothing, until eventually the sentence was revived, and the phoenix of black letters returned to the page to put an end to the torture of this ungodly prose.

...eek out the path your Father has carved for you.

Therein you will find both darkness and light.

In an unforgiving cycle.

I snapped the notebook shut. I wanted to discard it, to toss it into the nearest bin and never think about it again. But there was something in those words, a familiarity to the prose that was far too close to be a coincidence. I'd read similar words before, but in the moment their location was something I could not quite place. It was as if a dark cloud lay over that part of my mind, making the memory difficult to navigate. There were fragments, half remembered, just out of reach, something similar to the feeling of déjà vu but not quite the same. It wasn't whole, a jigsaw with only the edges available, and felt almost incapable of ever being filled. As I studied the words closer a cold chill swept over my body. I recognised the handwriting. The curl of the letter e and the crooked crossing of the t. The handwriting was mine.

I sat and baked in the sun of the afternoon trying to dispel the dread of the contents of that god-awful notebook, waiting for my bus home. I was so distracted that I didn't notice the clean-cut man in a suit walk up and sit next to me at the bus stop until he spoke.

"...hello, friend. Would you like to know the good news?"

Even though his manner seemed to be without hostility, there was something within that sentence that felt like a threat. I didn't reply, hoping that he would simply move on and bother the next person he came across. I clenched my fist, just in case.

"...Jesus loves you, and he wants you to be saved."

It was then I saw the flash of the badge attached to his jacket.

Elder Michael

The Church Of

Jesus Christ

Of Latter-Day Saints

My fist unconsciously unclenched and it was already scratching the back of my head before I noticed the release in tension. I wanted to tell him to fuck off with such certain bluntness it would be impossible for him to believe he could traverse the conversation in such a way to win me over. I wanted to tell him that I didn't think Jesus existed. Or if he ever did, he was long dead and never coming back. Or if he did still permeate through human existence in some sort of sentient, yet no longer physical form, he clearly didn't give a single shit about any of us. Though these responses would have no doubt ended the interaction between the two of us, returning me to my dismal silence, avoiding the inevitable back and forth of "Why does God let bad things happen?" to "Well he works in mysterious ways" that occurred with conversations between the blindly faithful and the immovably faithless, I instead remained silent and let Elder Michael wait for a response that would never arrive. After the awkward silence had set solidly into the moment, Michael continued with his diatribe, perhaps unaware, but most likely without naivety, to the fact that I cared less than a little about what he was spouting. Michael read as if from a script, practised until perfection to the point that the entire speech was nothing more than a monotone drone of pre-rehearsed verbiage devoid of any shred of emotion.

But then mid-sentence Michael stopped. He paused, looked around as if to check that no prying ears or eyes could be party to the conversation, and then shifted slightly more towards my position.

"Look, I know you think what I'm saying is just bullshit. I get that. I used to have my doubts too. I know there's nothing I can say that will change your mind, but if you saw what I have then maybe you would. So, let me ask you this... what if I'm right? What if what I believe is the truth and you miss the chance for redemption? What if being so closed off to the idea of divine salvation causes you to miss the train to nirvana, the gates of heaven closed to you for all eternity? What if you never got to see the people you love, the ones you've lost, ever again? Surely worth at least a little thought, right?"

He looked away into the distance behind me.

"I think this may be your bus. Please just think about what I've said, Sheldon."

He stood and flagged the bus down, before extending his other hand towards me. I stood as the bus pulled in and shook Michael's hand. He smiled warmly. I got on and sat at the back as the bus drove away leaving Michael behind in its wake. I sank back into my seat, unable to get those final words he'd spoken to me out of my head. Not how he told me of my potential damnation if I didn't adhere to the word of his saviour, but instead dwelling on his very last statement.

"Please think about what I've said, Sheldon."

I never told him my name.

III

There are many things I remember from when I was young and many things I don't. I remember sitting in my dad's car listening to Jonny Cash with him. I remember that the CD deck was broken and when the final song of the CD played it skipped on the outro, repeating a riff or vocal line depending on the song. The Jonny Cash CD my dad had burned and played more than any other was not exempt from this curse, with that last "ring of fire" sung by Cash being repeated over and over again. This would continue ad infinitum if not for the short sharp blast of my father's fist on the dashboard which caused the CD to reset itself, the riff of Folsom Prison Blues clarifying that the cycle had started again. Every time this happened my dad would let out this almost painful near-muted laugh, as if this process reminded him of something traumatic he didn't want anyone to know.

I don't remember my mother. She died a few minutes after giving birth, leaving my father and her brother to raise me, until there was only my uncle. I don't remember much about the day my dad left, most likely because I was unconscious in a hospital bed.

In the town I grew up in there was a museum that had an exhibition on Ancient Egypt. I'd gone there with my primary school for a trip once and fallen in love with the place. I made my dad take me there almost every weekend. I remember he enjoyed it too and was obsessed with one of the displays, a small sapphire rock in a glass case with a plaque that read "The Heart of Apophis." Every time we went there, he would stare at the display for at least ten minutes, placing his hand on the glass when no one was looking, closing his eyes and breathing deeply. I never thought much about it at the time but in retrospect it was strange, although most of the things my dad did were odd.

He'd bought me the Horrible Histories book on the subject of Ancient Egypt and I'd read it every night. I'd become absorbed in documentaries on the subject, even ones that were intended for an audience way beyond my years. I remember the first myth of that era I ever read, that day and night were not merely a passage of time but actions of the gods. That every night the goddess of the sky would swallow the sun-god Ra, only to give birth to him every morning. I loved how the Ancient Egyptian's viewed death; the belief that not only the spirit, but every sensation of a human's earthly being, was taken to the afterlife. The jackal god Anubis and the decision as to whether a person was worthy determined by weighing their soul against

47

that of a feather. That deep within the Earth's core Osiris lay waiting, the god of the underworld, the deity of death and resurrection, that such a great power could exist below my feet with the potential to bring back the dead. I remember one day digging in the back garden with the small red trowel I'd got as part of a children's gardening set birthday present, attempting to get to the centre and meet Osiris. I'd been digging for at least an hour when my uncle came to ask what I was doing.

"I'm digging to the centre of the world so I can bring back Mum."

Tears filled his eyes and he turned to the kitchen window. I hadn't noticed it before, so had no idea how long he'd been there, but my dad was stood looking through that window directly at the spot where I was digging. My uncle motioned with

48

his hand towards the hole, his eyes set harsh upon my father.

"Are you not going to do something about this?"

My dad walked away from the window and came outside. He didn't say a word to my uncle. He merely scooped me up in his arms and carried me into the house. Before he placed me down on the floor of the front room he whispered in my ear,

"I got close, but I didn't get deep enough down either."

I'd always been an incredibly hyperactive child. There was a worry that perhaps I had ADHD but the tests came back negative. My attention wasn't at fault, when focussed on a task I became wholly engulfed by it, but when left to my own devices I would run rampant through the house as if powered by some infinite energy source. I would create fantasy worlds to live in, the four walls of whatever room I occupied transforming into a different universe of my own making, but always inspired by the Egyptian gods. On the day my father left I was in the kitchen while he made Sunday dinner. It was my birthday too, all I wanted was to eat the home-made pyramid shaped birthday cake my uncle had crafted, but my dad insisted we ate a proper meal first. While he slaved over steamed vegetables and sliced beef, my uncle was arguing with him about something. My attention was within my own imagination, though occasionally a phrase would penetrate the armour of escapism, temporarily disrupting my immergence with talk of this not only being my birthday, but another important day that my father had completely neglected. At the time I didn't realise exactly what my uncle was talking about. I was too young to make that connection.

Deep in my fantasy, playing the role of Horus, son of the great god Osiris, I fought the evil god Seth for the throne as king of the gods. I was in the heat of battle while my dad poured boiling water over gravy granules, ignoring the scorn of my uncle. I fought Seth tooth and nail, yet although evenly matched he landed a hard kick to my chest, sending me hurtling backwards. I hit the lino, my head flinging backwards, my occipital bone meeting the hard floor with an incredible thud. I jumped to my feet, a deep rage festering inside me, and ran across the kitchen to enact my revenge. In the mythical world of legend created within my mind, I flew across the air, released an almighty war cry, and landed a powerful kick into the chest of my enemy. The same happened in the reality of the kitchen, but my enemy was instead the cheap wooden cupboards near to where my dad was cooking. Though in a world of fantasy, the anger I felt and the power of my kick were very real, so much so that the cupboard door split from the aggression of my attack. My real-life uncle must have said something that had deeply antagonised my dad, because at the same time as my war cry he screamed at full volume, not any words but just an animalistic howl of pain and frustration, before banging his fist down onto the counter with great force, his strike in complete synergy with my own. My uncle stepped back from my father in shock, mouth agape, my dad's reaction clearly a much higher magnitude than the argument warranted. The combined force of the two impacts not only dropped me to the lino once again, but caused a Richter-Scale tremor through the cheap wood, causing the fecklessly placed measuring jug of scalding hot gravy to vibrate with enough force that it lost its flimsy footing on the cabinet top and toppled haphazardly onto my head. The naivety of youth forced me not to cover myself but instead look up, directly towards the brown magma raining down on my face. I thought I noticed my father turn and watch this unfold without care, as if he were viewing a series of actions he knew were going to happen yet didn't want to change. I feel like I remember him observe the gravy scorch my skin before turning away without the slightest hint of concern, even as my uncle began to dive in complete panic towards me. I have an image imprinted in my head of the last seconds before I lost consciousness, but it's one I refuse to believe. My memory is hazy and doesn't come back into focus until late that evening when I was already bandaged and had been heavily sedated to reduce the pain, but I swear in the final moment before I sank into unconsciousness I saw my dad smiling.

The doctor explained that had it not been for an experimental new process, that had only recently passed the trial stages, I could have been left with some heavy discolouration and severe scarring across my face and torso. Instead I would still have to deal with these issues but on a much less severe scale. If everything went well, the affected areas would look like they were "merely in a constant state of mild sunburn," as the doctor put it. For eight weeks I was expected to stay in hospital while they bandaged and re-bandaged my face daily, soaking the skin each time with this secret new ointment. But when the bandages were removed for the first time I looked exactly as I had before that boiled liquid hit. I left that hospital without a single iota of proof of what had happened on my skin, as if the entire incident never occurred. No one could explain it, they'd approximated months before the redness would begin to dissipate but there I was, only a day into the treatment, as pale and pure skinned as I'd ever been.

The last thing I remember before I blacked out was my dad, the complete nonchalance in his expression changing just slightly as his lips arched into a smile that seemed to convey a long-forgotten understanding. This would be the last time I would ever see my father's face, at least in the flesh. He had fled from our lives as the ambulance took me to the hospital, my uncle unable to drive so riding in the limited room of the van with me whilst my dad claimed that he would follow behind in his own car. My father never made it to the hospital, leaving my uncle the only remaining guardian of the boy who, less than an hour before he vanished forever, had lay burned to the bone, slowly convulsing in shock on the kitchen floor. The car was eventually found miles away near some caves, and returned to us, with no trace of my father. The police searched for some time but without a single lead; they gave up without giving any closure as to whether he was dead or had simply abandoned us. Though a constant reminder of his leaving, we kept the car and my uncle started to take lessons so we could make use of it.

There was an affliction of my trauma that remained, however. Every night since the accident my dreams had become infinitely more vivid, often making it difficult in my younger years to be able to draw lines between what was real and what wasn't. My nightmares began as if they were reality, I would be sat in class at school or watching television in the front room at home. But soon that comfort would shatter and I'd be surrounded by nothing but black, chased through pure darkness by a creature with headlight bright yellow eyes before falling into a vast body of water, unable to swim due to an invisible weight pulling my body down deeper into the depths of nothingness. I would wake crying in the mornings and try to cough up the gallons of imaginary water that felt trapped within my lungs with such force my throat would be sore for the entire day. It would take me hours to calm down, and days at school were often filled with the terror of uncertainty as to whether I was awake or still asleep. I got better at this, or at least with dealing with the aftermath of its effects, but the dread throughout the morning after one of these dreams never truly left.

My uncle raised me for the most part of my life. Having been now involuntarily thrust into the role of father figure with no idea how to raise a child, my uncle always felt and acted more like a big brother. There was definitely the feeling of protection, a security that comes with the love of a parent, but there was also a cool friendliness to his persona too. Not so much a lack of all authority, but more an open understanding of the need to occasionally break rules. The first time I had come home drunk I was fourteen, just before I unintentionally drifted away from the few friends I had and became more alienated. We'd got some cheap cider thanks to an older kid who used to go to our school. After giving him the money we waited down the side of the shop for his return. He was at an age where he could get what we needed, without being too old to pass judgement against us. I'd returned home from the park and was greeted by a small black cat without a collar sat outside my house. He stalked over, meowed with want, and then rolled onto his back to expose his underside. I lay there with that cat for a while, stroking its belly and enjoying the feeling of inebriation for the first time in my life, until my uncle opened the door to find his nephew drunk on the concrete with a no doubt flea-infested stray.

"Get in."

That was all he said. He sat me down and poured water into me until I sobered slightly. He never shouted, and never really judged, but his actions and his manner were far from condoning. After a while he looked me up and down and motioned towards the stairs. I began to head up and without looking in my direction he said,

"You better not piss the bed."

We both laughed and I swayed gently on an ocean of now decreasing intoxication until I reached my room and passed out, fully dressed, on my bed.

My uncle only ever spoke about my mum and dad once, because I only ever asked him once. We'd spent the day fishing, something I had zero interest in but he'd insisted. With nothing but silence counting down each agonising second of stillness I decided to scratch an itch I'd had for some time. I'd never asked about my parents because I was afraid of what the answer might be, that perhaps my imagined fantasy of who they were was much better than whatever might be lurking in the cold dark caverns of the truth. I was also afraid that opening that dialogue would affect my uncle negatively. If he was okay with talking about it, surely he would have done so by his own volition, but he never mentioned them before I asked and he never mentioned them again after.

"Your mother was an angel. Don't get me wrong, when we were young we fought from time to time like kids do. But every time, even when it was my fault, she'd be the one to make amends. I remember once she'd broke the head off one of my toys, only by accident, and I screamed and yelled at her and she just stood there and took it. She must have only been four at the time. I said I was going to cut the head off her favourite doll, and she didn't try to fight back, as if she felt she deserved it for her mistake. But like I say, it was just an accident. Anyway, I'm sat in my room sulking when I hear this knock at my door. It's your mother, my sister. She's taken the head off her favourite doll and tried to tape it onto the body of the toy she broke. I mean, it looked god-awful, a real freak show, but the fact she sacrificed this thing she loved just to make amends…. she was an angel."

We sat in silence after this, only the gentle ripple of the water causing vibrations in our ears, until my uncle once again split through the calm with his words.

"I don't know about your dad. No one did except your mum. He sort of came from nowhere one day and then he just stayed. It's hard to explain. I'm not even sure how he and your mum met. It was

61

just all of a sudden, she came home and there was this guy that she was with and she wanted to move in with. Hell, I'm not actually all that sure she knew much about him when I think about it. But she could always tell if someone had a good soul. She said your dad did and that was enough for me. I liked the guy, but he had an awful temper at times. I think he knew it though and he tried a lot to keep that in check, he always seemed so ashamed anytime he lost it. I think your mother felt bad for him because deep down she knew he was a good person. She got him meditating and all sorts of stuff. He always thanked her for that, said that without her he'd be a different person. We were never really close, your dad and me, and he pretty much flew off the rails again after you came along and your mum..."

He trailed off not wanting to associate the two events even though it was impossible to separate them. My birth and her death were eternally fused, and every birthday I had was a constant mirage of happiness and celebration for him, hiding the pain and brutal fact that the special little boy blowing out the birthday candles was the reason that she was dead. I'd pieced this together over the years, but this was the first time it had ever been confirmed. I tried ignore the lump in my throat in order to spare the awkwardness my uncle was presumably feeling.

"...anyway, we only really ever had one real conversation. You know, one that lasted more than a minute and wasn't an argument. I don't know if I ever told you this, but before you were born I studied archaeology. I even got my masters in it, but I never really did anything after that. I guess I should have, but life has a way of veering you off in directions you don't expect."

He paused and stared off across the water for a few seconds before shaking his head and coming back into the moment.

"What was I saying? Right, the time me and your dad had a real conversation. Well he found out that I'd done my master thesis on ancient cave systems in England and began to ask me all sorts of questions. I didn't know he gave a damn about that kind of stuff until that day, but we spoke for easily over an hour about my research. He had some really strange ideas about this stuff, and when I told them what he was saying wasn't possible he'd laugh and say about how there's stuff in the world that seems impossible until you experience it yourself. You like Ancient Egypt, right? Did you know that if you stand next to the pyramids the increased gravitational pull from their huge mass actually slows down your perception of time? It sounds wild, and it's so slight it's pretty much unnoticeable, but your father told me that, so I checked it out and it's right. He took that and created this notion that if you ventured deep enough into the core of the earth eventually gravity would become zero, because there'd be an equal pull in all directions, and this would make time irrelevant. Well, maybe not irrelevant, but it would be a place where the linearity of time didn't exist. Now I'd only studied archaeology, but your dad was asking me about some bizarre stuff about physics and the nature of time. I told him that wasn't even close to my field of knowledge, but that it'd be impossible for a human to ever travel that deep without it resulting in death. He laughed before shaking his head and just walking away like I didn't know what I was talking about. I couldn't believe it. He'd asked me and then mocked my response. He mocked the knowledge of factual science. I did like the guy, like I said, but he was one of the strangest people I've ever met. I don't truly understand what your mother saw in him, but she did seem happy before she…"

My uncle trailed off again but this time we sat a little while longer in the silence before my uncle once again spoke, the calm air the catalyst for a chemical reaction brewing inside him. A chemical reaction composed of the urgency to not leave the final thought on the connection between my life and her death, and to finally confess to something he'd kept hidden for nearly a decade. "Your dad left a note for you. Just before he left. He scribbled it down and sealed it up and told me to give it to you. I didn't want to, at least not until you were older. Shit, I don't think I ever wanted to give it to you. I don't know what it says, I never looked. But it's still there if you want to. I'm sorry I didn't tell you sooner, kid. Your dad had been acting really weird leading up to that day. I don't think he'd really been okay since your mum passed. But he was acting really odd the few weeks before he went. I'm really sorry. I know I kept this from you, but I just didn't know what to do. I didn't want whatever it is he wrote in there to mess you up."

We stayed for a little while longer, catching no fish but not really caring if we did, before we headed back home. I hadn't told him whether or not I wanted to read the note, but he passed it to me anyway soon after we'd got back. I expected something like a note from my missing dad would have some physical weight, even if that weight merely came from a psychological manifestation, but holding it in my hand it felt light as air. I stayed up late with my uncle, talking little and watching whatever dumb shows were on T.V. before eventually heading to bed. It was there, in the dark of a room illuminated only by the light of a weak bedside lamp, I read the words that my father had left me. The only thing he had left before he mysteriously vanished. I split the envelope and then pulled out the tatty piece of note paper from the envelope, unfolding it to reveal its secrets.

I must return to where I was led

By the path my Father cut out for me

And start again

In the Creswell Crags

Where the Devil cannot pass

I was consumed by darkness but you my child

Just like your mother

Have always been the light

In this unforgiving cycle.

IV

It had been just under a week since I'd met Mara and I still hadn't called her. Merely wanting to see her did not feel like a valid enough reason. Fortunately, that day I received an email asking if I was available to review a local battle of the bands competition at one of the pubs in Manchester that was happening the next day. It was arguably the most well-known Heavy Metal venue in the city except Rebellion, and I used to joke that the bouncers would let you in based on how much you looked like a Viking. I'd been in there once before, watching Ten Foot Wizard, and asked at the bar if they served coffee. I didn't realise I was asking the owner, who for some unknown reason, took umbrage at that request. She leaned over into my face and said, "No. We're a pub not a fucking café. If you want something other than beer you can piss off elsewhere." So, I wasn't a huge fan of the place, but it seemed a decent excuse to finally call Mara. I'd been putting it off for days, yet was unable to get the idea of seeing her again out of my head. It had been the worst of both worlds; the guilt of wanting without the satisfaction of doing. I'd spent hours just staring at my phone, pacing the room, trying to build the confidence to call and then backing out, retreating from the desire to talk with my tail tucked between my legs. I felt that, at least with the excuse of being given a plus one for entry to the show, I had a reason to ask her out other than simply wanting to see her. This was obviously the way of a coward, and I felt great shame in my lack of confidence.

The phone rang out for a long time and I was close to hanging up when she eventually answered. I hadn't given her my phone number, but she answered by saying my full name. I wanted to apologise for not calling sooner, to explain the delay was not born out of mere dismissal but a deeply rooted sense of guilt that wasn't logical but incredibly emotionally powerful. I wanted to explain why I had backed away when she tried to kiss me, and tell her about the way my body seized up when she held my hand. Even though it had been incredibly uncomfortable for me to feel close to someone again, I wanted to push past that barrier and break the walls of that dam. Instead I merely said that there was a gig I was going to. I didn't even ask if she wanted to join me, I just allowed a long silence to hang until she picked up the thread of the conversation and did the work for me.

"I will meet you at the Town Hall at twelve thirty. We can do something before the show too. Okay?"

I agreed and hung up. A surge of anxiety coursed through me with such force I had to sit down and breathe deep for a few minutes. I remembered how when back before I'd quit drinking completely, a shot of whiskey would ease the anxiety slightly. I missed having that crutch at hand, my ability to settle hindered by a sober restlessness, and I could not place the exact reason I'd quit. I knew that alcohol once had a hugely negative impact on my life, but I couldn't remember what the climax of that realisation was. Once I had managed to control my breath, I was struck by a feeling of claustrophobia. The small dimensions of my flat seemed even tighter around me, so I walked the streets near my home for an hour until I felt calm enough to return home and try to sleep.

V

My awareness sparks into life like flickering embers rekindling into a new fire, absorbing the oxygen around and illuminating everything that was previously darkness. My toes curl around the edge of the soft dirt under my feet, feeling the lap of the tranquil water before me. A vast lake sprawls out ahead, its berth covering my whole field of vision. The land surrounding is dark, but the lake is bright. A moonlit glow beams up through its waters as if that grand luminous orb was resting, submerged deep within. I exhale, and a fog of icy breath hangs in the air before dissipating into the nothingness surrounding me. The earth groans. A tectonic shift from below causes the ground to tremble. The lake darkens and the calm that once was begins to ripple until a crescendo of violence erupts, disrupting the peace and causing the ebb and flow of the waters to become increasingly tumultuous. An air of dread fills the area. An apocalyptic ambience like the subtle bass tones of a horror movie score, the knowledge that something evil is coming. The lake begins to bubble as steam emanates from its surface; the violence ever increasing, the dread constantly growing.

Something was nearing the surface.

I awoke drenched in sweat. A human sized pool of perspiration soaked the sheets of my bed. I tried to shake away the looming sense of disaster that had resulted from the dream as I showered and dressed, but the feeling would not remove itself. Its claws stuck deep into my flesh whilst it constantly pecked at my brain, a feral crow of trepidation that refused to release its grip. The one benefit of this feeling, the silver lining of this god-awful storm cloud, was that it was a distraction from the thoughts of anxiety surrounding my meeting with Mara. My focus was wholly on the remnants of the nightmare, and by doing so any fear of the potential intimacy of the day were quashed, pushed aside by that lingering dread.

I met Mara at the Town Hall. I arrived five minutes before the time agreed, she appeared fifteen minutes late. She apologised and I dismissed it; fifteen minutes was nothing really. We walked down towards a building called the John Rylands. It was an old library that was built at the end of the eighteen-hundreds, but after being opened to the public it had become more of a museum. It was the building across from the café Mara and I had sat the morning after I met her, and we mentioned then how nice the gothic architecture looked, so it seemed a good spot to visit for our second meeting.

We walked down towards the building, but no gust of wind blew Mara's hand into mine this time. I was glad to see her, but it was clear that whatever rejection she had felt last time had caused her to be a little more cautious with her affections. I knew I wouldn't be the one to reach out and hold her hand, no matter how much I wanted to, and I realised I wanted to quite a lot. I was a coward, or I was trapped by whatever feelings of guilt I had, or perhaps a combination of both. I walked with my hands loose in the air, hoping she would repeat the gesture and link us physically. Mara walked with her hands deeply buried in her pockets.

The entrance to the building was also its exit, so the gift shop was the first thing anyone saw when they arrived. It was filled with a series of curious and macabre gifts, as there was currently an exhibit named Magic, Witches & Devils in the Early Modern World. The items for sale seemed to grab the attention of Mara, who ran towards them with the giddy delight of a child. She'd pick up each one individually and explore it thoroughly, placing it down gently with an affirmative nod or almost slamming it back into place with a highly audible tut depending on whether the product satisfied her or not. I merely stood a couple of steps behind her and watched with intrigue as she did so. Sometimes when she slammed down an object her hair would lunge forward and fall across her face. Mara would take one hand and pull the hair back into place, wriggling her nose in the way that she did during the process. The exhibit featured a number of incredibly old manuscripts, books and other items detailing a belief in the supernatural the world around. Mara would often laugh reading these, and she told me that she'd had a fascination with all things mystical since she was young. We entered one of the rooms and there was no one else in there. Mara ran off in one direction and I went in the other, looking at each piece but not really absorbing anything. There was something in that room that shocked me however, though I doubted its validity. In a large, glass cabinet there was a small square of paper, barely larger than a thumbnail, with what looked like Hebrew text but was so faded it was almost indistinguishable. I read the info plaque and it claimed that this small shred was in fact a piece of the oldest surviving Christian Bible. I called Mara over with an excitement I hadn't shown the world in a long time and she bounded over, mirroring my eagerness until she realised what she was looking at and her face cringed into one of disgust.

"I hate this Bible."

She then did something that paralysed me in shock. She picked her nose and then wiped her finger along the clear glass containing the shred before emitting a fake spit, audible but with no fluid, towards the floor and walking immediately out of the room. I stood there frozen in place, unable to process what the hell had just happened, mouth agape.

I found Mara outside the John Rylands. She was leaning with her back against the glass of the entrance, smoking a cigarette and tugging at the sapphire stone around her neck. Did she smoke last time we met? I tried to rummage through the archives of my brain to project our previous meeting across the cinema screen of my mind, but I couldn't quite grasp that memory. I didn't think I'd seen her smoke; surely I'd remember a detail like that. I tried to conjure an image by taking the plume of thick, grey smoke billowing out of the mouth of Mara, and supplanting it into the hours when we sipped coffee, in the hope that creating this false image would somehow spark into life a real memory, but my attempts were in vain. Whether she had smoked or not was unclear. She smoked now, that was apparent. When Mara noticed me, she dropped the cigarette to the ground and crushed it under foot. She smiled in such a warm way that it made me momentarily forget about how insane the last few minutes had been. Mara grabbed my arm and forced it into an arch, placing my hand on my hip, an involuntary handle created so that she could then place her own through the empty space and capture me in a link.

"I would like a drink."

Her statement was followed by a stern nod, and then I was dragged forcibly towards a nearby pub called The Rising Sun. The place was practically empty. There was a middle aged woman tending bar, and one man sat in the corner who looked so old he could no doubt remember when God was a child. Mara fished out a handful of coins from her pocket and pointed to the jukebox.

"I pick the music, you get the drinks. Deal? I will have rum and coke."

Before I could reply she was already at the jukebox, feeding it coins and tapping her finger against the screen.

I ordered a rum and coke. The lady behind the bar dropped two large cubes of ice into the glass before pushing it up into the optics to release the dark brown liquid. She placed the glass onto the bar and then reached into the fridge, pulling out a glass bottle of coke. Perspiration ran down the bottle as she popped the cap off and placed it next to the glass of rum. It looked so good I ordered a bottle of coke too. The bar maid offered me a glass with ice, but I refused. I've always thought drinks tasted better in a glass bottle.

I sat down waiting for Mara to finish with the music. She bashed the screen with the same infantile glee as she had running towards the gift shop in the museum. There was such a joy and innocence in her every action and seeing her that way caused that deep-rooted grief to manifest itself in my consciousness once again. She sat down just as her first song began to play. I couldn't pinpoint the band but I had heard the song, and I could tell from the thick familiar accent that whoever it was were from Manchester.

I don't have to sell my soul,

He's already in me.

I'd lived in this city my entire life, yet still I knew nothing about the most famous music to come from here; the glory days of Manchester music. I cared nothing for The Smiths, and I tolerated Joy Division at best. I guess that made me a poor journalist. Knowledge of music should have been my oxygen, but I only really cared about the heavier stuff.

Mara closed her eyes and swayed her head side to side to the music, before snapping back to a sudden alertness and pouring the coke into her rum until the glass nearly overflowed, the ice cubes dancing seemingly in time with the music too. She arched her neck forward like a giraffe at the water hole and sipped the drink until it was low enough to be lifted, and then took a large gulp before setting it down and staring perplexed at the other bottle of coke on the table.

"Where is your drink?"

I knew what she meant but I merely pointed to the bottle and smiled.

"You would make me drink alone?"

I apologised and explained that I didn't drink. That I hadn't drank since... when did I stop? The question once again emerged out of the murky waters of my mind. I knew it had been a long time, but I still couldn't pinpoint the moment I stopped or what catalyst brought to life the desire to live in complete sobriety. I shook my head mid-explanation, unable to finish my reasoning, instead I just repeated the statement.

"No, I don't drink."

Mara kept the puzzled look on her face for a few moments before shrugging it off and taking another large gulp of her drink.

"You probably think I'm weird for what I did in the museum."

I wasn't sure if it was a question or a statement, but the truth was that I'd already forgotten it had happened. If she hadn't mentioned it right there, I don't know when I would have remembered, but with it fresh in my mind the vast chasm of curiosity had opened up and swallowed me whole. The scene flashed through my mind once again, as vivid as when it had happened, but I still couldn't fit the pieces together. Mara's reaction had been so sudden, so visceral, that something tragic must have happened in her life to evoke such a response to a single shred of paper encased in glass. I didn't know how to word my eagerness to peel back the seal and discover the motive behind her actions, and the air hung heavy with silence until Mara decided to tell me the story anyway. She swallowed the remaining liquid, the ice crashing together like colliding glaciers as she set the glass on the table. Mara wrinkled her nose the way that she did and exhaled.

VI

"I lived in a very small village in Romania. There was not much there; basic farming, a little church, many goats, but nothing more. There were seven of us, my father and the six siblings. My father was a great man, a man of science, but the people of the village didn't understand. Romania was still a very religious country, and a very simple country too. This was a bad combination for my family, as the people did not like migrants, especially those with ways different to their own. My father would conduct experiments in the woods at night, he did so to avoid any attention as the people of the village were already suspect of my family. I lived in the village, but I wasn't born there, I did not come from Romania. We had travelled a lot and settled here because of its quiet solitude. We thought we could avoid the changing world and live simple lives. We were wrong, and the simplicity of these villagers would be our downfall. One night a young couple were out in the woods. They had to sneak out because they were siblings and their family would not take kindly to the things they were doing. My father was out there too, working on an experiment, when these two caught him and decided his science was in fact devil worship, black magic. Can you imagine? These two are out fucking in the woods as brother and sister and they think my father is the one committing sin. You would think the whole village would exile them for their behaviour. But no, this was a religious village and fear of the occult and in dark magic was still rife. The couple told the priest they had seen my father in the woods trying to summon demons, and the priest believed them with no evidence. The priest had a wife, who was very beautiful and kind, and nothing like her husband who looked twice her age and found only grievance in the joy of others. The priest ruled the village, everyone was afraid of him, everyone except my father. My father would cure the sick with medicine, and the priest would accuse our family of witchcraft. Until this point, however, nothing had been done and we'd been left alone with nothing but gossip in hushed tones whenever we walked by. Now the priest decided it was time to act. He had two witnesses to my father's activities and that was enough in his mind for prosecution. He demonised my father in front of the entire village in church, saying he was in league with Satan and attempting to drag the rest of the village to hell. We never attended church as we were not Christian, so my father never had opportunity to defend himself, and his verdict was decided before he knew he was on trial. The villagers liked my father, but they feared the priest more. They banged upon our door, threatening to burn our home with us all inside if my father did not come out. We begged for him not to go, but he said he had no choice, that he would not let harm come to his children, and that he could not stop the flow of fate. Before he left, he kissed me gently on the forehead and it felt as if he was giving every iota of his love to me in that one kiss. It felt like electricity; a giddy thrill shot through my body in response to the kiss but then I was left only with pain. I knew that he was being taken to his death. They tied my father up and dragged him into the village square. Although my father pleaded for us not to, my family followed. They beat him until he struggled no more. The priest began to scream biblical verses before stabbing my father through the heart with a wooden stake. They must have thought he was a vampire or something like that; it was a belief that many in the country still held. My father lay dead in the street; the man who had shown me the world and cured the village of the sick countless times was now gone forever. They covered his body in salt and made a bonfire over his corpse with sticks. They burned my father before my very eyes. I tried to cry but I could not; it was too unreal to be true. My siblings and I held each other while his body was burned to ashes. The fire was still burning as we escaped into the forest, fleeing from the monsters that had destroyed our lives. We heard rumours that they had kept the fire burning for seven whole days as part of this ritual, to ensure whatever evil they thought my father possessed had been completely cleansed from the world. This is why I hate the Bible. It has stolen everything from my family and forced us to live out in the wild like dogs. I spit on that book and all it stands for. I wish for anyone who believes its lies to feel the pain that I have felt because of that stupid, goddamn book. I wish every single one of them dead. They believed they were killing my father in the name of God. For me and my family though, this was the day that God died."

She wiped the tears from her eyes and let the anger in her speech subside.

"You can choose to believe me or not, I just wanted you to understand."

She grasped the sapphire stone around her neck and lifted it slightly.

"This necklace my father gave me; it is all I have left."

Through the entire tirade that flooded from Mara's lips, it felt as if I was listening to a different person than the one I had met and pulled from the toilet cubicle of Rebellion. The awkward shyness and curious glee I had seen up until this point was gone. In front of me now was a fiery beast filled with anger and resentment born from pure malice against the people that had wronged her in such an unthinkable way. She didn't seem human when she spoke about what happened to her family. She was wrath manifested. It was strange to hear her talk like this; she had seemed very easy spirited.

Beneath all of that anger though, there was a deep and endless pain. The pain of a little girl who had lost her daddy. It was clear the weight of her father's death had left her broken, far more than could ever be repaired. There was something odd about her last sentence, though. It was strange that she'd given me the choice as to whether or not I took her word as truth, clearly wanting me to believe her and show her understanding, but aware of her unfathomable story. Perhaps she would have doubted its validity herself if she wasn't the one telling it, if she hadn't seen her father burn before her eyes. I tried to picture Mara as a child. A small girl raised in a small village, her family ostracised by the community for some reason that didn't make sense to her and losing the person she loved more than anything else due to the superstitions of the people she had grown to trust. It was a daylight too harsh for a young girl to bask in, and I could only imagine the damage it left at such a young age. I looked at Mara and saw all the pain of the world compressed into this young woman. I understood why she held such hate; what else could she feel for those who took what mattered most away from her? Behind her smile and blasé demeanour, there had to be an unfathomably deep well of anguish. When you've been robbed of the man who raised you, it's hard not to hate those who took him. It's hard to finally turn your back on that hate even when your world does eventually expand and the better seeds of humanity, the realisation that not everyone is a monster, become dispersed and start to take root within you.

My mind flashed a memory, triggered by the thought of Mara's family and the loss of the man that raised them, transporting me to the details of a day I thought I remembered perfectly. I was once again sat by the riverside with my uncle, asking about my parents. The speech was the same but at the point where the memory would usually stop, where my uncle told me about my dad, there was a skip like the needle on a record jumping two songs ahead. Suddenly I was in front of the TV with my uncle, watching whatever dumb shows were on. He'd handed me the note my father had left me but at this point I hadn't read it yet. When I recalled this memory, we usually just sat there in silence until eventually heading up to bed. Every detail of the memory was in the same place, except this time, he turned to me and spoke.

"There's something I want to tell you about your dad. Something he said to me. Like I say, and I don't mean to badmouth him, but I don't think he was really.... okay, mentally. Like something wasn't right in his head. He only told me this once; it was late and he just came into my room. He was usually pretty quiet, but this night he woke me and told me so many things that were just unbelievable. I don't know if I should be telling you all this really, but..."

Another skip on the record and I'm in the kitchen. It's late, the light of the moon a slight illumination across an otherwise darkened room. I'm stood on the cold lino flooring looking down at the shape of my uncle. He's covered in blood and doesn't seem to be breathing.

VII

I'd sat still while Mara had told me the tale of her upbringing, not even noticing that her broken English had completely vanished during the entire story. My mind only paying attention to the sudden flash of seeing my uncle dead and bloodied. The shock of that image caused me to knock my chair back, and I shot up as if the ghost of his memory was a physical spectre before me. My face white and panicked, I looked around the room lost and overwhelmed. Whatever psychological dam my brain had put up to keep that memory locked away had now burst, the furore that came flooding out was too much to handle. My head was rushing with blood and adrenaline, the room spinning furiously.

"Are you okay, Sheldon?"

I couldn't respond. Mara was close enough that I could reach over and touch her face, but my mind felt no longer attached to my body, her voice sounding like the fading ebb of the last remnants of an echo. Fight or flight kicked in and the latter easily won. I exited the building without a word, the intensity of the sunlight only adding to the surreal feeling of complete detachment from reality. I swayed like a drunk back the way we had come, towards the town hall, stumbling into an alley and vomiting on the floor. I saw thick, red liquid burst from my mouth and hit the floor, spattering across my shoes. I sat, crumpling to the floor like a ragdoll, in the alley and tried to breathe deeply in an attempt to calm the adrenaline and stabilise my vision.

Once I'd settled slightly, I thought about going back to see if Mara was still there. Mara, having done nothing wrong but open her heart to me, must have thought it was something she'd said. I slowly raised myself to my feet. I looked down. To my relief I had only vomited my breakfast, not blood. A second wave of anxiety flooded over me, spurred by the thought that my own mind had tricked me into believing I had puked blood, that my own mind was seemingly out of my control.

The idea that my thoughts and feelings were not being controlled by myself, but by some unknown force deceiving me into believing these false images, was terrifying.

I got up, still slightly off balance, and began to walk. I was aimless, focussing on merely placing one foot in front of the other and not on any sort of direction or destination. I still couldn't focus; it was as if a switch had been flicked, and whatever darkness had been sealed behind the locked doors of my mind was now free to fester inside my psyche and run havoc. The air around me felt heavy, with the peculiar sensation of purely internal symptoms having such an effect that they seem to alter the entire atmosphere of the external world. The image of my uncle haunted me; I was unsure if what I had been shown was real, or just some fragment of a nightmare my brain had stored incorrectly as a memory.

The sunlight of the day was bright and it hit me like a severe hungover. I continued to sway, blocking its light with one hand over my eyes, my head down, bumping into people as they passed, completely oblivious to them or their reactions. It was then that I felt a hand from in front of me grab my shoulder hard, making it impossible to proceed forwards. I took away the shade of my lifted arm, my eyes gradually adjusting to the light to see Michael stood in his same suit, name badge glinting in the sun.

"Sheldon, Sheldon, it's me. Look at me. Are you okay?"

I tried to focus on his face, but I was still unsettled. He didn't ask again and instead took me into the shade and placed me down onto a bench. I didn't resist this movement, not that trying would have achieved anything. I was guided entirely by Michael's will until he released his grip and sat down next to me. My head fell into my cupped hands, my elbows landing onto my knees.

"Just breathe. You're okay. What happened?"

I didn't explain the events, just the sensations I had felt. A long list of poorly described symptoms tumbled out of my mouth and Michael nodded understandingly after every single one.

"It sounds like you've had a panic attack. You're okay, you're not hurt. It doesn't feel nice, I know, but it'll pass and you'll feel normal again."

I knew all this, of course. I'd had plenty of panic attacks and plenty of advice on how to deal with them, none of which usually helped. There was something soothing in Michael's tone however, and sounding like a live version of an ASMR recording, he brought me back down to earth.

I turned and smiled, still doubled over.

"Don't think just because you helped me I'm gonna start loving God."

Michael let a little chuckle out into the air, stifling it quickly as if even laughter was a sin, before placing his hand on my shoulder again, this time with a gentle touch.

We sat in silence for a while, probably only a few minutes but it felt much longer. Michael shifted his position and sighed.

"Listen…"

He paused, re-evaluated whatever sentence was meant to proceed after, and instead asked me to explain again what had happened in the moments leading up to him bumping into me. I explained, this time not omitting the narrative of events, and when I mentioned Mara his demeanour seemed to drastically change. His jaw clenched, he became agitated, appearing impatient for me to finish my story so that it was again his turn to talk. I wound it up, and as I hit the last syllable of my tale he stood up and turned to me, folding his arms.

"You should not spend time with that woman. I've seen you with her and she's bad news for you. You need to distance yourself immediately."

I was shocked by his statement and responded with anger.

"Excuse me? You've seen me with her? Are you stalking me?"

"You don't understand. You don't know who she is. I know her and she's bad news. I'm looking out for you, Sheldon. I promise I only have your best interests in mind. Please keep away from her. Promise me."

"Get fucked, you creep."

I stood, feeling the strongest I had since the panic had hit. I walked up to Michael and got so close I could feel his breath on my face, so close I swear I could hear his heartbeat increasing as he prepared for whatever I was going to do. I spoke quietly but firm, a low tonality with the heavy bass of authority, with only enough volume that these words were his alone.

"You're gonna stay the fuck away from me from now on. I don't know what your game is, I couldn't give a shit. But stay the hell away from me."

I walked past Michael, with no destination except as far away from him as possible. He didn't move, but simply said my name with a such suddenness it caused me to stop.

"She was an angel. You know that don't you, Sheldon?"

I should have just ignored him and kept walking. I was seething with rage that my personal life had been invaded by Michael. I wondered how long he had been watching me. Did it start when we spoke at the bus stop? Or it had begun even earlier than that? The mystery of his words kept me glued to my position, the question impossible not to ask.

"Who was?"

He looked me straight in the eyes.

"Emma."

VIII

It was a hot Sunday morning in the middle of July. We drove around the tight winding roads of Snake's Pass with the windows down. Emma's feet were on the dashboard, her shoes were off. She wore a pair of socks I'd got her online, a pack of three with each pair showing a different scene from a Studio Ghibli film. They were styled in a basic pixelated way, like an old Super Mario game. Today's socks were Spirited Away, and Emma would pull them up at regular intervals so that the images were always on show. The music playing was a collection of pop-punk songs from the first decade of the millennium, back when we were both teenagers. Some of the songs I recognised, dragging me back to an age of bad skin and insecurity, others I wasn't so sure. I hadn't made the CD that was playing, so every new song was a complete mystery to me until it blasted from the speakers and reached my ears. At the end of each track, as the music slowly faded to silence and the sound of the engine resurfaced, Emma would turn to me from the passenger side, eagerly awaiting the first chords of the next song, to see if my face showed any sign of familiarity with the sounds flooding the vehicle. Some I recognised, most I didn't. We'd stayed over in Sheffield the night before at a place called The Harley. It wasn't any sort of luxury hotel, but it offered cheap rooms near to the centre and that was enough. It wasn't as if we'd be spending any time in the room, it was just somewhere to sleep after the gig Emma had dragged me to. This happened a lot, Emma would persuade me to come to watch awful bands who were now in their thirties yet still sung about high-school crushes. Admittedly, last night hadn't been another of those "aging men still clinging to their youth" ensembles. That evening we'd watched a young girl armed only with her mellifluous voice and piano to accompany her. I welcomed the change, and enjoyed the music more than I'd expected to, but I still acted the same and feigned a begrudging willingness to participate. I'd roll my eyes and act like my agreement was a huge favour on my part, but the truth was that I didn't mind because I was happy just being with her. I really enjoyed driving around the country with Emma, regardless of the reason. She gave me a strange comfort that I'd never really felt with anyone else. Though I never said it, I hope Emma knew deep down that these little adventures we had meant everything to me.

There's this Freudian notion that every man searches for the characteristics of their mother when choosing a partner. I never knew my mother, my only connection being a handful of photos, so I couldn't search for characteristics. It was a pretty strange idea, the Oedipal Complex, but I was aware of just how much Emma looked like my mother. Maybe there was something to it, that the absence of my mother caused me to fall for someone with a striking similarity in looks as a way to fill that void. But my love for Emma was far more than just surface level; I'd grown more enamoured with every moment we'd spent together. I joked once that she was the reincarnation of my mother, her spirit in a different body. I think that was one of the only times Emma didn't reply with a sarcastic remark to something weird I'd said, she just shot me this perplexed look I'd never seen her make before and I never saw her make again. As we continued to drive along Snake's Pass, I turned to Emma and smiled, remembering how we first met.

I'd just come out of the hospital. The doctors had said it had been a miracle that I survived. My memory of it all was not vague, that wasn't the right way to describe it, certain elements seemed crystal clear in my mind, but others were completely missing. It was more like a jigsaw puzzle with only the edges in the box. I could work some fragments, but the picture was incredibly incomplete. I'd had no one to come and get me, so the doctors let me go once I'd fully healed and they were satisfied with my condition. I think the car must have been totalled, or maybe it wasn't my car that had been in the crash, either way my only way of getting home was the bus. There I was, fresh out of hospital after a near-death experience, a sardine in a metal box on wheels being thrown side to side with every bump or turn as the above capacity vehicle crawled through the rush hour traffic. I was sat near the front of the bus, on one of the few seats that weren't occupied by other travellers, and spent the journey looking at nothing in particular, just staring through the legs of all the people who were forced to stand, without any focus. The bus jerked again as it had a hundred times already, but this time Emma fell like the rain straight into my lap. She flicked her blonde hair around as she twisted her head towards me, smiling as if she'd meant all along to turn me into her impromptu seat.

"Well, hi! Come here often?"

She beamed an ear to ear smile without showing any teeth, her eyes squinting as she did.

"Not often at all, but I'm glad I did today."

I didn't notice it right away, but I was smiling back at her. An incontrollable smile, the kind that almost becomes a chuckle. Emma giggled at my response, and her chuckle quickly became full blown laughter.

"That was so cheesy! I thought my opener was bad but bravo, sir. You win that round."

She never got up, we sat there talking the entire bus ride, completely unaware of the whispers and stares of the people around us. She was dressed in knee-torn skinny blue jeans and a bright yellow t-shirt that fit tight around her upper-body. The book under her arm had the word PHILOSOPHY in bold print as the header, and there were some larger loose sheets of paper with hand-written scrawls jutting out of its pages. There was an image of a man with a huge moustache on the cover and I remember thinking that could be any damn philosopher as they all seemed to have a thing for big facial hair.

Emma crossed her legs and the bottom of her jean leg lifted slightly, revealing a tattoo of a chemical formula.

"That's serotonin, right?"

Her face lit up with my observation, her entire body vibrated with excitement as if this was the first time anyone had noticed the origin of her body ink, and maybe it was.

"It is! Do you study chemistry? Or biology? Or medicine or something?"

"Oh no, it's just the state of my mental health is absolutely shocking."

Emma burst out laughing and the few on the bus who weren't already staring at our antics now did. Her laughter had been involuntary, something she couldn't contain, and her expression instantly turned to one of apologetic regret for laughing at my statement. I smiled hard, looking deep into her eyes with reassurance, and then we both began to laugh hysterically.

Even though we were merely inching through traffic the bus ride seemed to end too quick, the old adage of time flying was true, it had gone right out the window and left me wishing I lived even just a few stops further down the road.

"This is mine."

I shuffled to stand up and Emma hopped off my lap, standing in my way and blocking my exit towards the front of the bus. She pushed her hair back with a single flick of her hand, and I noticed a biro pen placed haphazardly atop her ear. She shuffled, looking towards the ground with a previously unseen shyness. Without a word she grabbed my arm, pulled the pen from behind her ear, and wrote eleven numbers on the back of my hand before signing them with her name and a small love heart. Then Emma kissed my cheek before sitting back down in the seat I had occupied without another word. I didn't know what else to do, so I laughed awkwardly and got off the bus without even saying goodbye. When I got home, I waited an excruciating few hours before I decided it was socially acceptable to text her. She replied almost instantly, and we arranged to meet a few days later.

There was a bar in Manchester centre that offered food, beer, and bowling. I had no idea what constituted a good date, and hadn't planned anything before meeting her, so that seemed like a good shot. Emma seemed genuinely happy when I suggested it and put her hand up to high five me. I lifted my hand in response but at the last second Emma shifted out of my way and laughed as I missed my target.

"You've got a good first date game, I'll give you that. But now you've gotta earn that high five."

We ate a burger each and drank two beers before we bowled.

"That book you were reading, the philosophy one, who was the guy on the front?"

"Oh, that's Friedrich Nietzsche."

"Is he the God is dead guy?"

This question made Emma laugh hysterically.

"Yeah, he's the God is dead guy."

"Who's your favourite?"

"My what?"

116

"Your favourite. You're obviously into it pretty big so you must have a favourite?"

"It's not like picking your favourite ninja turtle, you prick! But I guess I like Descartes a lot. Not him as a person, he was a bit of an arse, but he had this idea about an evil demon that exists and tricks people."

"Wait, an actual demon?"

"No, I don't think so, I'm not sure. Though he did dissect his wife's dog because he believed some wacky shit about dogs being machines because they didn't have souls, so Christ knows what was going on in his head. But I think with this it was more like something within ourselves, something deep and dark that can deceive us into believing things that aren't true. Or, at least, he put forth the notion that our minds have the potential to trick us. Like, we're sat here drinking and talking but how do you know

117

you're not drugged up in a ditch somewhere? Your brain, well not your brain because you're a dope, but brains are pretty powerful things. So, what you believe to be reality, or your memories, or whatever, might not be actual external things you're perceiving. They could just be something within our own minds, like an internal vision, if that makes sense?"

"Not one fucking bit. But you're very cute when you get so passionate."

"And you sound like a complete dick head when you say patronising stuff like that."

Emma pulled her tongue out at me, as if the tone of her voice wasn't enough to indicate she wasn't actually offended, then downed the rest of her beer before walking over to the bowling lanes in a pretend strop.

As I expected, I was terrible at bowling and was pretty sure I'd never been before or, if I had, it was so long ago that my mind had merely got bored with holding on to that memory and dumped it into the part of the brain where all the never to be used again information goes. Thankfully Emma was just as awful, and the evening was spent tossing balls into the gutter and laughing at how ridiculous we must have looked. We drank a couple more beers before we left and then headed to the bus stop. Emma laced her fingers into mine on the walk down and gave my hand a little squeeze.

"Sheldon, I have a favour. It's dark now and I have to walk through a park with a lot of trees to get home. Would you walk me home?"

"Yeah, of course."

"But it's not an invitation. I'm not a first date kinda girl, you perv."

She laughed and I did too.

We got off the bus at her stop and I walked her through the park, her hand once again locking mine in its grasp as we strolled through the trees. I never got to her front door, Emma released her grip at the top of her street and said,

"This is mine. I had a lovely time tonight. If you don't call me for a second date, I'll kick you in the balls."

She raised her hand for a high five and I raised mine again, awaiting either the rejection or the harsh slap of skin. Instead Emma gently interlocked her fingers around mine and kissed me. Her free hand worked its way to the small of my back while my non-prisoned fingers danced through her hair. After the kiss Emma reached down and squeezed my butt before dropping one last peck on my lips and walking away. Halfway down her street and without turning she shouted,

"You earned that!"

Even though it would take me an hour, I decided to make the rest of the journey on foot rather than wait for the next bus. I smiled the entire way home.

I brought my mind back to that day on Snake's Pass, where it took me three whole seconds to snap back after Emma screamed my name. It was in those three whole seconds that my entire world was destroyed. I'd heard that if you saw an animal in the middle of the road you were meant to hit it rather than swerve, that doing so was the safer option. I wasn't sure if it was some sort of urban legend without any real legality. No one I knew had ever been told this from a driving instructor, only hearing it the same way someone hears a piece of unexciting gossip, blindly accepting its premise simply because it seems so mundane to be any kind of fiction. I'd heard this, and even though after the crash I would think that perhaps yes, hitting that goat may have averted the whole fucking disaster, in that moment where I snapped back to reality after my wandering mind had taken three seconds to respond to Emma's cry of anguish, my brain didn't recall that nugget of information and instead reacted on impulse. Turning the wheel hard to the left and swerving out of control, we smashed through the road-side barrier and hurtled over the edge. The car began to flip violently down the hillside, the two of us trapped inside and screaming with pure terror, before crashing into a lake. That's all I remember, a few moments of complete panic before the car hit the surface of the water and life changed forever.

When I came back to consciousness Emma was already dead. I was told by the paramedics that she'd died before they'd pulled us from the lake, probably from the impact as we'd hit the water. That I should take comfort in the fact she most likely would have died quickly and without any kind of long drawn out pain. I was told that there had been no hope of resuscitation, and that it had been a miracle that I'd survived unscathed. It had been one year, three months, and eight days since that day on Snake's Pass. I'd taken three seconds to react to Emma's voice, and because of that I'd never hear it again.

IX

I wanted to leave. I wanted to continue walking away from Michael and hope to Christ I never saw his face again. How did he know Emma's name? Had he really been stalking me for that long? There were so many questions that had arisen from him simply uttering her name to me. Though I wanted to be strong enough to expel them from my mind, move on, and forget this whole interaction, I wasn't. The sound of her name weakened me. Took me back to every moment, every time our hands would meet, every early morning kiss, every joke and the laughter that followed, every fuck, every argument and every making up, until the world decided to take her from me. The lump in my throat was of gargantuan size, impossible to swallow and restricting my speech. I opened my mouth, but without words there was only hot breath. I turned to Michael, walked slowly towards him, and stood there in silence. Whatever was to follow was to be led by him. I didn't want to give him any prompts, for fear he was some kind of cheap palm reader, utilising cold reading tricks to garner small nuggets of information and using them to his advantage.

"You don't remember do you, Sheldon?"

A silence hung in the air until Michael realised there'd be no answer to his vague question and re-started his line of inquiry with something more specific.

"How did you meet Emma?"

"I'd just come out of the hospital."

"Right. And why were you in there?"

"I'd been in a car..."

A bright flash shot across my mind along with the realisation that the memory wasn't correct. Emma had died in a car crash, that's how our story had ended, but it wasn't how it had begun.

"I'd just come out of the hospital. But I can't remember why."

"It's important that you remember. It'll help you understand what's going on here. But you need to remember, I can't just tell you. I can guide you, Sheldon. But only you can open the door."

"There was an accident, not a car crash but something else. I'd been in the hospital for a long time, but I don't remember being there. Just coming out."

"Okay, how about this instead. What's the last thing you remember before coming out?"

Another flash. My uncle on the kitchen floor. Bloody and unmoving. White lino stained red. But I could only see him and the immediate space below him, not what was around him, the rest of the scene blocked from my view. Had I been attacked too? Perhaps someone had broken into our house, maybe a burglar who didn't expect anyone to be home? No, that wasn't it. I tried to recall what had happened, but it was as if that area of my brain was surrounded by giant thorn bushes. The more I tried to get to the information the more the thorns dug in, causing my brain to scream with pain. Michael took my shoulder and sat me down.

"You're almost there, Sheldon. Take your time."

The picture in my mind of my uncle's deceased body lying on the floor was clear. I could see the details as if they were there before me. As if not remembering but observing a Polaroid print of that night. But it was a two-dimensional image, one that I could not scan around. I tried instead to think not about what was going on around me, but what was happening within me in that moment. My attempt to call forth the emotional response of that night had a different effect. Instead of giving insight into how I felt that evening, it gave me a glimpse of my physical form. There I stood, over my uncle's body, naked except for some loose-fitting boxer shorts, blood across my torso, knife in hand. I remembered an argument with my uncle, but the details of it I couldn't quite reach. There was something about my father, or was it my mother? It was too hazy to remember the specifics, but I remember pushing my uncle backwards into the kitchen cupboards. He got his footing back and though in my mind I could see his mouth scream words at me, there was no sound. Whatever those words were, I couldn't recall them no matter how hard I tried. I saw myself reach towards the knife rack and grabbed a handle, the one at the top right, the largest blade. I saw myself screaming back towards my uncle, waving the knife. I saw the shock and fear in his eyes. The sound of the memory cuts back in just in time to hear my uncle say what would be his final words.

"You really are your father's son."

In a blind rage I plunge the knife into my uncle. Three hard stabs into his stomach. He staggers back a single step and hangs in the tension for a few seconds before crumpling to the floor. There I stood, over my uncle's body as his last moments sputtered out on the cheap lino floor. The realisation of what I had just done set in and I fell to my knees and began to wail.

Another flash. Back on Snake's Pass with Emma's feet on the dashboard. I look at the radio clock and it says that it's three in the afternoon. I'm driving over the speed limit and I'm drunk. I look at Emma. She's crying, her eyes are flooded with tears.

"I don't understand why you get so mad at me. I really don't know what I've done. I don't deserve it Sheldon, I really don't. I know you've had it bad, but you can't keep taking it out on me. It's not fair."

"I'm not taking shit out on you, Emma. You're overblowing the situation completely."

"Overblowing? Sheldon, we had to leave the concert early last night because you were screaming at me for some reason I still can't quite figure out. You just switch from this loving and caring man into a complete fucking monster and I never know what it is I'm supposed to have done wrong. Then you

130

completely vanished, left me to walk back to the room alone, in a city I hardly know, and you don't come back until three in the morning. I didn't know where the hell you were or if anything had happened to you."

"I was fine. You don't have to worry about me."

"I do worry about you, Sheldon. Especially when the first thing you do when you wake up is drink."

"I only drank this morning to stop the hangover. I can't drive hungover."

"There's always a reason, always an excuse. You shouldn't be driving when you've drank in any situation, Sheldon. I'm shocked you even think that's a valid reason. I can't believe I actually got into the car when you're like this. Shit, I'm just as bad for letting you get behind the wheel."

I have no response. The music continues to release up-tempo melodies as I swerve around the narrow bends, but the atmosphere is far from sanguine. There's noise from the stereo but the whole car feels cloaked in silence. Emma stares out of the window for seconds that feel like months, before turning back to me.

"I think you should go back to the doctor and talk about getting some kind of counselling to go with the meds you've been taking. I know you like to handle things yourself, but I think you need a little guidance, professional guidance. And you need to stop with this constant drinking. It isn't good, it isn't the right way to cope. It's a short-term salve that you're just perpetuating until you eventually spiral into total fucking oblivion. I have to be honest,

Sheldon, I hope you don't get mad. I love you, I really do. But you're killing me. The rage, all the drinking, it's too much. It never used to be like this, I don't understand why things have changed. You were so different when we first met. You used to say that I'd saved you, that because of me you could put all the darkness of the past behind you. For a while I believed that, but you clearly haven't and I don't know what to do. I don't think I can save you again, Sheldon. It hurts me so much to say this... but if this is the path you've chosen, then I don't want to be dragged down with you."

I turn and look deep into her eyes. I don't know what to do, how to pull myself out from this abyss, but I can't lose her.

"You're right. I'm sorry. It isn't anything you do, I promise. I just lash out at whoever is nearest when I feel like this. Emma, I'm really sorry. The last thing I ever want to do is upset or hurt you. I don't want to keep doing this, keep being this person. You did save me, you have saved me. I've just lost my footing. I don't know why, I've just felt like the universe is swallowing me up. I've got this constant feeling of impending doom, like something bad is going to happen and I can really sense it, as if I'm tuned into it. I know that sounds stupid, it probably is. I can be better, I swear. I'll talk to the doctor, I promise. Emma, I..."

"Sheldon!"

I fell off the backless bench, hitting the floor with a thud and shocking Michael to his feet. He reached out his hand to help me, but I batted it away, creating distance between the two of us by scuttling backwards like an injured animal. The fear in my eyes silently screaming the horrible truth. I'd murdered my uncle and killed the woman I loved.

"Sheldon, it's okay. Just breathe."

But I didn't want to. I wanted to close that door in my mind once again. Push the demons back in and forget they ever existed all over again. I knew I couldn't, I knew this time the door had been blasted off its hinges. An irreparable breakout of the one thing I'd spent so long in a mental hospital trying to deal with. They didn't call it that though, such a phrase as mental hospital would have all sorts of negative connotations. Junction Thirteen's Unit Eight was an "in-patient adolescent mental health service" and while I was hardly a child when I entered, even less so when I left, I wasn't yet legally an adult. It probably worked in my favour, being so young. Instead of just being sent to a prison for the criminally insane to become nothing but one of the poor, crazy bastards that society couldn't handle, I was placed in an environment with the hope of rehabilitation and an actual future. I couldn't remember clear details of what had happened in the couple of years I'd spent there, but simply recalling the name of the hospital filled me with a strange chill, the kind only the horror of a past traumatic experience can provide. Though exactly what had occurred within the walls of that building still eluded me, I knew that my recovery hadn't been easy.

For so long, instead of coming to terms with everything I'd done I'd just pushed it into a corner, sealed it away, and hoped it would never see the light of day again. The question still remained of exactly how Michael knew all this, but the squall of remembrance took precedent over anything else. I'd killed my uncle, and they'd put me away for a long time because of it. I still couldn't remember my time in the hospital, no doubt blurred by whatever cocktail of drugs had been funnelled into my system, but other pieces began to fall into place. I hadn't just left the hospital the day I met Emma; I was just returning for a check up to make sure everything was okay. Instead of incarceration, they'd decided on a long period of medication and therapy to which, it seemed, I'd eventually responded positively. Upon leaving the hospital I'd been provided with a few things to help me get my life back together. I'd been given the all clear, but I'd killed the only form of support that would have been available to me, so the state had to step in to fill that void. A small flat above a sandwich shop and the first year of rent payments upfront, as well as any additional financial assistance needed until I became a productive member of society again. It seemed strange to be given so much when weighed against the reason I'd been in there for so long. I still had to take a bunch of pills every day, that I do remember, and I know I stopped taking them once Emma died. I remember early into our relationship

Emma had encouraged me to send some of the music reviews I'd written to a website I'd been reading for years, and how good it felt when they replied positively and asked for more. I remember feeling, for a time, that whatever proverbial light at the end of the tunnel there was for me was almost in reach, until my life went hurtling off the roadside and crashed into complete darkness again. I wanted so much to just give in after Emma died, to let the pain consume me wholly and suck me into whatever oblivion lay waiting for me. I remember how writing reviews was the only thing that kept me from falling completely off the edge. Emma had been so supportive about my writing, it felt like it would be an insult to her memory to give that up. I remembered the car that had once been my father's, and then my uncle's, had then passed to me. This metal box on four wheels had been a constant reminder of two people no longer part of my life, until eventually it became the coffin for a third. I remember buying a cheap second-hand car after Emma died but being unable to drive it, overcome by acute panic anytime I sat in the driver seat. It would still be in the small garage that came with the flat as far as I knew, I hadn't looked in there for months, the keys discarded in a drawer with old takeaway menus and instructions for white goods. These memories came flooding back, but they were scattered, not formed into a linear timeline, like the shards of a dropped glass on the floor. It was difficult to fully decide what happened and when, but it was a little clearer. The crash I thought I was in before I met Emma was the one in which she died. The reason why no one was there when I left the hospital was because I'd been in there for killing the last member of family I had. I wasn't sure why, but I remembered the term "random manic episode" was something that was said often to me while I was at Junction Thirteen.

It was a lot to process in one influx of information. Michael was still stood over me, his hand of empathy still outstretched and waiting to save me from the current of dread trying to wash me away. But I didn't want to be saved. I didn't want understanding. I didn't want to get past these issues and grow. I wanted to forget. I wanted to shut myself away and forget about Michael, about my father and uncle, about Mara and Eytan, and just have my memories of Emma. I missed her like she had just died all over again, and the realisation that I was to blame for her death was a weight too immense to bear. I wanted to go back to my flat, lock the doors, draw the blinds, and cease to exist in the real world. I'd killed everyone who mattered to me, and if I ever did get close to another person I'd no doubt ruin them at best, and destroy them at worst. I just wanted to be locked away with my memories of the only woman I'd ever loved. I didn't even deserve that, to live the life of a recluse. I was a disease, a curse, a virus. I was the bad omen before a storm. The world was better without me.

I struggled to my feet.

"I'm sorry, Michael."

I left, Michael still standing with his arm outstretched until I turned and walked away from whatever potential salvation taking his hand could have held.

X

I sat in the driver's seat of a car I was unable to drive. There was nothing but silence, the walls of the garage blocking out whatever outside noise could have potentially seeped through the slits in the rusted steel doors of the Ford Focus. There was no music, the radio player broken. I allowed my mind to wander, trying to imagine at what point it had ceased to operate. Was it long before, or had it sputtered out after it came into my possession? I remember the middle-aged lady who had sold the car to me. Her kindness had extended beyond just the low price, she had also offered to drive it directly to my door. She'd offered a test drive before I gave her any money, but I trusted her word and refused. After the paperwork had been filled, after we had waited making small talk until her husband picked her up, only when the two of them had drove off did I sit in the car. I put the key into the ignition and as life flowed throughout the vehicle, that was when the panic struck. Intense flashes of Emma's face smiling at me, Emma's face as she screamed my name, Emma pulled out of the wreckage, no longer breathing. I couldn't even drive it the few metres up into the garage, tears running down my face as I pushed it into its eternal slumber. I considered selling it on, but I didn't see the point. Mere pennies for effort I didn't want to make. So, there it sat, covered in cobwebs and rusting even more. Having remembered so much, I wanted, but was unable, to cry or scream or vomit out the anguish that felt trapped in my chest. The key was resting on the dashboard. I'd opened the door and sat in with no intention to drive, just festering in the silence with an inaudible pressure in my ears. When you spend so much time trying to block out your own thoughts, your ears suffer for it. Not used to silence, they ring with white noise when finally met with a noiseless air. So many people are uncomfortable being alone in quiet thought, without the infinite distractions available in life. For a while I wasn't either, constantly fearing what psychosomatic creature might crawl up into the forefront of my mind. But only now, I found a strange solace in the inner hum that came with external silence. As much as the wall of my brain had finally been torn down to let the horrors be revealed, there was a comfort in knowing that I no longer had to fight against myself. I no longer had to keep caged Descartes' inner demon that Emma had spoken about on our first date. The sins of my past were now my present, it was who I was and there was no erasing that. I was accepting the pull downwards into oblivion and letting it consume me wholly.

I'd become so absorbed in my homespun, sensory deprivation chamber, that when my phone pinged with a text my entire body let out a startled spasm. I spent the next few moments trying to work out just where the hell the noise was coming from.

"Can you work tonight?"

The clock at the top of my phone screen read 20:42. This was the latest I'd been asked to come in. It wasn't the first time I'd received late messages, but these were usually for the following day. I wanted nothing more than to just sit in this little box, to keep the world away, but Eytan had done so much for me it felt wrong to refuse. Without his odd jobs I wouldn't have been able to pay the rent, so I felt as if my sadness was not a valid reason and I decided to accept, to try to brush off the cobwebs of melancholy the best I could.

"Sure."

I got out of the car with heavy effort. I didn't bother to lock the door, didn't bother to go back inside my flat. I just left the garage and walked right to the bus stop with the perfect timing of a well-structured plan, as the bus turned the corner seconds after I started to inspect the timetable.

The evening was barely illuminated by natural light when I got off the bus. There was a strange pink and orange glow, but that was quickly succumbing to the darkness of night. A warm air with a suffocating pressure filled my lungs. I prayed that the cold temperature of the coming dark hours would fill the streets and allow me once again to breathe. Manchester is a city that is never without a crowd, finding even an unmanned back-street a near impossibility. Tonight, Deansgate was desolate however, not a person or vehicle in sight, and I walked the entire road down towards Rebellion with the eerie silence my only company.

I knocked at the door of Rebellion, checking the time on my phone after I did. It was 21:43, not early or late enough for the venue to be closed, so it was strange to see the entire place cloaked in total darkness. The noise of a key jangling around in the lock dispelled any thoughts I had about the place being empty, and Eytan opened the door without a smile.

"Well you look happy to see me."

He let out a single "ha" which, by Eytan standards, meant he'd found genuine amusement in my joke. He didn't usher me inside, instead walking away without a word until I took the hint and followed him into the main room. I still had the heavy weight of sadness upon me, but not simply wallowing in that pain, being out of my flat and somewhere I felt comfortable, filled me with a slight semblance of normality. I asked what the work was, and why the place was shut at this time. Eytan simply ignored my questioning and tapped at the screen of his phone. After a few minutes he slipped it back into his pocket and finally turned to me.

"Come, there's something I want to show you."

He led me towards the STAFF ONLY door I had never before entered. I was curious as to what exactly I would find behind there, complete disappointment filling me when we entered into a small square room with nothing but a computer and small desk in the corner. The paint on the wall was coloured off-white, as if it had been painted decades ago and gradually faded. Eytan leaned over the computer, avoiding the available chair, and began to try to bring the screen to life. He bashed some keys and slammed the mouse down hard a few times, before trying with a little less aggression, eventually coaxing it out of standby.

"Sit down. Look at this. It's from the other night, the gig you worked."

I sat and looked at the screen. There were four equally sized squares showing different areas of the venue, with the exception of one which was completely black. I could see the entire stretch of the venue on one, the entrance on another, and on the third the room we were now sat in. Eytan banged about with the keyboard and mouse for a little while longer until the three screens jumped back to the gig. I expected him to point out someone in the crowd to see if I could identify them, maybe there'd been a theft or someone had damaged something, but instead he fast forwarded through the entire evening and paused it after a few hours had cycled through. Frozen on the screen was an image of me and Mara lying asleep in the otherwise empty main room.

"What's this?"

He didn't respond. He just clicked play and then walked out of the room, leaving me alone with the footage of the two of us sleeping playing on the screen. It wasn't soon after he'd left that something started to happen. One of the motionless bodies began to move, at first just the usual twitches of slumber, but eventually these twitches became more severe, until I was looking at my own body convulsing with incredible violence until it stopped abruptly. The screen was motionless again for a few moments, then I watched my unconscious carcass sit upright with alarming speed, before clambering over the arms of the two chairs and walking into the corner of the room. For a while I stood there without action, head dipped slightly, the heavy breathing of my body visible on the monitor. The person on the screen, though it looked like me, was impossible to see as myself. The movements didn't seem like my own, the erratic manner completely alien. The body slunk to the floor, pulling something from its pocket before scratching at it feverishly. I tried to squint at the screen to get a better look at what it was, my mind realising even before my eyes had finished focussing on the image. I now knew exactly where the strange markings throughout my notebook had come from. This scratching at pages continued for some time until the hunched over figure tossed the notebook across the room without notice as to where it landed. It then returned to the makeshift bed, rolled over the arms and settled into a silent sleep once again.

I leaned back in the chair and ran both hands through my hair. I tried to interpret what I'd just seen in a way that made sense. I'd never really been prone to sleep walking, only having been told once by Emma that I occasionally murmured incoherent noises while I was out cold. Nothing about what I watched made sense, and the entire thing felt false, like poorly shot online footage attempting to prove the existence of ghosts. Then I thought about my uncle, and worried that whatever had happened then had returned once more, that this temporary psychosis I had once experienced was back again. If that was the case, I took solace that at least no one had been hurt this time.

I sat a while longer, just staring at the two bodies in repose on the screen, hoping to garner a little more to unwrap the mystery before eventually conceding defeat. I clicked escape on the keyboard, bringing the footage back to the present, barely realising in time to turn around that a figure in black was stood behind me. I spun around in the chair and was struck hard on the side of my head.

XI

My awareness sparks into life like flickering embers rekindling into a new fire, absorbing the oxygen around and illuminating everything that was previously darkness. My toes curl around the edge of the soft dirt under my feet, feeling the lap of the tranquil water before me. A vast lake sprawls out ahead, its berth covering my whole field of vision. The land surrounding is dark, but the lake is bright. A moonlit glow beams up through its waters as if that grand luminous orb was resting, submerged deep within. I exhale, and a fog of icy breath hangs in the air before dissipating into the nothingness surrounding me. The earth groans. A tectonic shift from below causes the ground to tremble. The lake darkens and the calm that once was begins to ripple until a crescendo of violence erupts, disrupting the peace and causing the ebb and flow of the waters to become increasingly tumultuous. An air of dread fills the area. An apocalyptic ambience like the subtle bass tones of a horror movie score, the knowledge that something evil is coming. The lake begins to bubble as steam emanates from its surface; the violence ever increasing, the dread constantly growing.

Whatever is approaching the surface is so close I can almost make out its form. A large dark shadow is moving underneath the water, it seems to be thrashing, as if it is unable to break out of its submergence. The shadow bangs against the surface of the water like a shark in a glass tank, causing thunderous crashes with each thrash. Eventually whatever barrier was holding it back breaks, and the thunderous noise amplifies a thousand-fold as it splits. Water shoots out like a geyser and floods my entire being. It becomes harder and harder to breathe as the water consumes me, filling my lungs until I can no longer choke out a single gasp for air.

    I slowly began to regain consciousness. I was on my back, that much I knew, unsure of my surroundings and unable to determine whether the darkness surrounding was actually the room or just a side effect of the blow I'd taken. I felt a dampness on the back of my head and began to panic, worried that the wetness I could feel was my own blood. My senses slowly began to return and with them came the knowledge that not only was the back of my head was sodden, but from head to toe I was soaked to the skin. I had no idea what had happened while I was unconscious, but it was safe to assume it wasn't anything good. Finally my vision gradually came back into focus, and I noticed that there were four figures dressed all in black in each corner of the room. It was too dark to make out anything other than their shape as they stood in silence. I tried to call out to them, but all I could manage was noiseless breath. I tried to stand and failed, having yet to gain full control of my motor functions; I had no choice but to lay on the floor in silence with the frustration of my weakened state. The sound of footsteps began their crescendo as they travelled closer to my body. It was hard to tell from which direction they were coming; the ambience of the room reverberated sound in a way that made it impossible to pin-point its location, until the footsteps came to a stop inches away from my left ear. A voice began to speak, and I recognised it instantly as the owner of Rebellion.

"I'm going to tell you a story, and you are going to listen."

The fifth figure in the room began to walk around while speaking. Though my entire being, body and mind, cried out to once again dip into unconsciousness, the words being spoken were so hypnotic it was impossible to detach myself from them and slip back into a blacked-out state. It was as if they had such a hold on me, that they were keeping me in a trance-like alertness.

"My family's history is a long one, older than written record. Many have theorised what we are, some have come close, but none truly understand our origin. A theory commonly peddled in the circles of tin-foil hat conspiracy theorists is that of the ancient aliens; beings from the cosmos that visited and granted mankind knowledge. This is the closest humanity has come to a correct answer, but they misunderstood one crucial fact. We came not from the heavens, but from the earth itself. Before the evolution of what you would call modern man, a civilization of advanced beings had lived for countless millennia on this planet. We existed before the arrival of our father, the great serpent of knowledge born from waters deep within this planet's core, but it was he who made us eternal. Do you know what lies deep within the earth? Seven hundred kilometres below, where no creature other than father has delved, there is a vast body of water concealed in a giant sapphire rock, called the Ringwoodite. The Ringwoodite was created by the immense temperatures and pressures of this planet, like a diamond formed by the atoms of compressed carbon, and within this trapped ocean lay an endless source of power, dormant since the creation of the universe. This ancient power was named the Leviathan. Sixty-six million years ago a meteor struck the earth; it wiped out nearly all life and caused the Ringwoodite to crack. This released the Leviathan and our father, the one who discovered how to flow through the waters of eternity, merged with this power and became one with the great serpent. Such power would have killed a lesser creature, but father absorbed it all and became a god.

There were survivors after the impact, though an incalculable number had perished. The few who remained banded together and decided what was to be done regarding the arrival of father. Though the wisest welcomed his coming; many balked at his presence, stubbornly refusing the incredible gift that had been placed before them, wanting nothing more than my father to be sacrificed to quell their fear. They were fools, every single last one of them. It is an embarrassment to think that these creatures could be so blind. With his power, father pulled the faithful from the ashes of the scorched earth, bestowing upon us fragments of his power and pushing us further than we had ever dreamed possible. The soil of the planet was barren and charred, nothing was able to grow, so father brought forth a great flood; a century long deluge to wash away the sins of the past to create life anew and eradicate the unfaithful. Soon after he decided to fill the planet with new thinking creatures, humankind. We, his children, were not happy with this plan. We had found comfort living among ourselves and did not want this peace disrupted. Father insisted, claiming that not creating this new life would disrupt the flow of fate. We, his loyal children, accepted his wisdom. After their creation we began to educate the troglodyte, and over countless centuries taught him how to become modern man. Over five thousand years ago, my people reigned over these creatures as royalty. We were physical gods individually named and worshipped devoutly by the humans. We began in what was once called Mesopotamia, what is now known as Iraq. We birthed them into existence, built their civilizations, and gave them the gift of language. We established ourselves as gods, and created religion to give their pathetic existence purpose, but their gratitude would not last. The world would soon see for the first time what could be described as war. These pathetic humans had begun to question the glory they had been given by us, to bite the hand that had given them so much. How ungrateful these little worms could be; believing their lust and greed for autonomy outweighed the need for the structure that had kept their existence in stability since their birth. The faithful were slaughtered in droves by heretics. Any person who still believed in our divinity, satisfied with our rule, was butchered in the so-called name of progress. We wanted to intervene, but father would not allow it, once again claiming that we should not try to disrupt the flow of fate. This war led humankind down a path of rebellion against everything we had gifted them, the aftermath of which destroyed the system of worship that had placed us above all other creatures. The humans were weak, stupid and unorganised, but they were many in number. We wanted to wipe every single one of them out of existence, but father insisted we merely move to new lands and start again. Heading west to the Egyptian realm, we took our knowledge and riches with us, carving our mark into these fresh landscapes and building another empire.

We once again placed ourselves as gods, merely rebranding to fit with the desires of the local tribes. My father, who had once been known by the Mesopotamians as Anu, took the name Huh and was worshipped by the faithful in the Egyptian lands much the same as he had been before. We told our origins to the people as something new, but it was merely the same myths and legends as before, just wrapped in different cloth. We have always been and always will be. Different names to suit the times, but the same story passed down for all eternity. We have given humankind so much, but of course we have taken from them too. Many sacrifices have been in our name, to maintain our position, sometimes by the hand of man themselves but just as often by our own. Father was never happy when we did this; the adoration for his creation clouded his judgement, but sometimes a necessary action for the greater good must be enacted, do you understand that?"

I managed to cough out a single word.

"Murder."

Eytan stopped his pacing momentarily, seeming to ponder deeply on what I'd said. As if it was a word he was familiar with but didn't completely understand the meaning of.

"Murder… yes, I guess you're right. There's no way around it. But…"

He paused again before resuming his marching.

"How can I explain? Do you feel guilt when you kill a wasp? You erase the life of a lesser creature so as not to inconvenience your own. Did you know that at the point of death, wasps have the ability to release a pheromone that sends other wasps to attack? Much like the wasp, humans are creatures of revenge. This is why we had to reincarnate into new gods in other lands. Without this shedding of our skin into a fresh form, the people may have become wise; followed the trail of our history and refused our rule. This would have complicated matters. Father wanted subjugation, not total annihilation. After all, humankind was his creation. So, at his wishes, this is how we operated for millennia; changing our names and our images to hide the blood on our hands from the people of the new lands. This was the only way to maintain any sense of structure, the only way to keep society stable. Without our methods there would be chaos; nothing but a multitude of primitive tribes butchering each other for all eternity. We created humans, but that doesn't mean we had complete control over them. I know you think this to be evil, but what you call evil we once called order. This was how we survived for so long; not as emperors or pharaohs in the open for the world to see, but from behind the curtain as the ritualistic dogma that was intrinsically linked to a system of religious beliefs. We were the glue that held together society, known through the manifestation of our desires into the images of the human's many gods. However, no matter how hard we tried, this was an order we could not maintain forever. Revolt would eventually flare in every society we created, and our hold soon began to crumble. The rebellion of Moses was the beginning of the fall for our people in Egypt. It seems that even gods cannot escape the flow of fate. It was not simply because the empire died, but because when it did the belief system we had created became scattered, fragmented, and slowly forgotten. We moved west again to rebuild. The Roman Empire allowed us to thrive for a time once more, taking new names as we had before, until the perversion of Christianity infiltrated and took siege of all we had created. Constantine, the coward, betrayed everything we had built and threw it to the wolves. Using our own methods against us, they created a belief system to counter our own, and destroyed our hold over society until there were no remnants left. The old gods that had been kept alive since the dawn of man now fell into the pits of their self-created hell, and became demons and devils.

Everything that had once been sacred was now anathema. There was no mercy for my family, and we once again had to leave. This time not to revive as a phoenix from the ashes, the cancer of Christianity too deeply rooted to cut away, but instead into hidden exile. This is how we settled eventually in Romania; a backwards little country filled with superstition. Their idiotic beliefs made them fear the old gods that were now their new demons, and at first this fear kept them at a comfortable distance. My family were viewed as witches and vampires; the things that come for you in the night and the things you should keep yourself and your loved ones far away from. Eventually we tried to live in harmony with these people, integrating ourselves into their lives whilst still being revered with a cautious sense of wariness, but the superstitions that kept them from our door eventually became problematic. These backward little people captured and murdered our father; the most powerful being that had ever been. Can you imagine such a fall from grace? To have once been the lord of the living world only to be slain by peasant farmers. To exist for aeons only to be destroyed by these pathetic excuses for creation. We took revenge, burning their village to the ground and cursing the survivors, to show them that any action towards us does not go unpunished. The people we had once lived with side by side burned in front of us, and it felt satisfying to hear their screams. After the death of our father, my family lived in solitude in the Hoia-Baciu; a simple and humble life but not the type of existence we deserved after all of our years of deification. We survived in the forest in total solitude, and prepared. The true history of our existence has been all but been erased. The true nature of our being deciphered only by a few, who are passed off as lunatics and ignored by the masses. Now we are ready to rise once more. We will make them remember who we are. The great serpent shall flood the lands once more and wash away the wicked."

Eytan's footsteps stopped right at my side. The room was completely dark, but I could feel him staring down at me.

I tried to get up onto my feet but was quickly knocked back down by the sharp pain of his foot in my ribcage.

"This is where you come in. The boy who destroys everything he touches. Your mother, uncle; every single person you've ever loved. You thought it was all a coincidence? No one has such bad luck. You, my good friend, are an anomaly. You shouldn't exist. You're a glitch in the matrix of human existence. Do you know that certain insects can exist without a father? They call them Hymenoptera, and they only possess the single set of chromosomes from their mother; half of a full being waiting to be filled. This is your affliction, but we will fill the empty space inside of you. The great serpent will rise once again."

Eytan crouched next to me, talking softly into my ear. The four figures didn't move; they were clearly a part of whatever was happening, yet Eytan seemed to almost shield them from his words.

"Mankind murdered our father many years ago, after he had given them so much. They didn't understand what he was and the great power he possessed. Like all the things those worthless creatures fear, they attempt to kill it; to erase it completely. But though the flesh died, my father's spirit cannot be killed. My father's essence is eternal; his soul not stemmed by the shackles of time. He is the great serpent, and he resides within you. All that remains is for him to awaken."

He grabbed a handful of hair from the back of my head and lifted me closer to his face.

"Now doesn't that sound delightful?"

I directed my glare towards the spot in the darkness that I thought was Eytan's eyes.

"Fuck you, and your great serpent."

He punched me hard in the jaw and my head flung back, smashing against the floor.

"It doesn't matter if your body is a little bruised, my father will still find it a comfortable home."

I spat blood into the darkness.

"What if I kill myself? There won't be a vessel then."

Eytan started to laugh, not the laughter of ordinary humour, something more twisted and sinister; the laugh of a man bent on chaos. It was impossible to believe what he was saying had any truth, the echoes of every brainwashed cult ringing throughout the four walls of the blackened room, but it was obvious that he believed it and would go to any lengths to see this to its conclusion.

"How naïve. That is the human in you, I guess. This is not something that can be stopped. As father always said, you cannot stem the flow of fate. You have been destined for this since your birth; it is encoded into your D.N.A. Your body has already begun its transformation. It began the moment you were born; a dormant seed that is now finally blossoming. Try to end your life and you will fail. Father will not allow it. He's already grown so much within you. Think back to your past, how everyone around you dies, yet you never seem to come to any real harm? This is not a mistake. There is no way you can stop this."

I heard the footsteps of Eytan begin to pace away from my body. I noticed a small horizontal line of dim light running part way along one of the walls. It had to be the door, it had to be an escape. I still felt weak, but if I was ever going to get away, then now would be my chance. I summoned all my strength in order to spring to my feet and run towards Eytan. He must have turned as I came towards him, because as my fist crunched into his head, I felt the distinctive features of his nose against my knuckles. I kept swinging until he dropped to the floor, and then ran my hands along the darkness of the walls in search for the door handle. The four figures still didn't move, and I wondered if they were actual people or merely mannequins, props in this perverse ritual. I was afraid of what their reaction would be, especially the one I was in closest proximity to, but they never shifted from their statuesque stances. My mind was a cacophony of panic and fear, yet I couldn't help but think about what Eytan had said about trying not to stop the flow of fate. Were these four figures allowing my escape? Was this merely non-intervention in the motions of destiny? I eventually found the door handle before I came to an answer. The light poured through. Although dim, it was still enough of a contrast to the dark of the room that my retinas stung. I turned back to see Eytan lying on the floor in his black robes. The four hooded figures stood motionless in theirs, with a bizarre series of symbols sprayed in red across the walls. There was also something sprayed onto the floor. A large glyph that covered the entire expanse, one that had recently become far too familiar. I recognised the infinity symbol and double cross motif, yet still could not place its name. I slammed the door behind me, leaving that ungodly scene behind.

XII

Each ring before Mara answered the phone echoed into the void and felt like a thousand stabs of fear into my gut. I was panicked; the torrent that was now flooding the streets only added to the urgency of finding somewhere safe, somewhere far away from Rebellion. My mind considered the idea that Eytan had dragged me outside while I was unconscious, which was why I'd woken up soaked, though I couldn't figure out what the purpose of him doing that would be. Then again, very little about his actions during the last hour had made any sense.

"Hello? Cheldon?"

"Mara, can I see you? Are you home? Something horrible just happened. I know it's late and a lot to ask, but... I need you."

Within fifteen minutes of traversing through the squall, drenched like a drowned rat, I found myself stood outside a tall building filled with the homes of what must have been at least two hundred people. I looked at the silver panel, the countless buttons all labelled with their respective numbers, and searched until I found the number Mara had told me. I pushed the button for apartment one thirty-eight and heard the distinct click and buzz of the door allowing me entry.

When I exited the lift onto the seventh floor, Mara was already there. She saw me, clothes dripping, and nearly laughed. She quickly switched her face to one of concern, clearly remembering the anxious tone of my ramblings over the phone. She took my hand and led me down a corridor, through a door, and into the privacy of her apartment. She pulled me towards the centre of the room, but I resisted, our hands parting as I turned and made sure that every lock on the door was in place.

Her place was small, but spacious enough for one person. There was a front room and kitchen within the main four walls, a door ajar that lead to a bathroom, a T.V. which was turned off, a single bookcase, and a small wooden ladder that connected to a raised area where her futon resided. I tried to scan the details of the room, but it was difficult to absorb anything with the adrenaline still coursing through my body. Mara walked behind me, and frogmarched me towards the centre of her living space before disappearing momentarily and returning with a towel. I stood there, motionless other than the small vibrations of my shivering, while Mara towelled me down like the owner of a dog who had been caught in a downpour.

I opened my mouth to explain, to detail the horrific happenings that had led to my panicked phone call in the middle of the night. I wanted to let Mara know that my anxiety had reason, that locking the door was not polite protocol but done with an incredible fear. Before I could release a single word, Mara placed her entire hand over my open mouth and smiled.

"I do not need to know the why. You are here and that is all that matters."

Her kind words did nothing to quell my trepidation. I began to run through the worst possible outcome that could stem from me coming here. What if I'd been followed by the four that were in that room? Perhaps I'd made a mistake involving Mara. If they were trailing me, if they

179

wanted to do harm, then all I had done by calling her was put her at risk. Mara, having done nothing wrong but open her heart to me, was now potentially in danger, a danger that I had forced upon her. She'd been there for me when I truly needed her, whether she was aware just how much or not, and all I had done to repay her was potentially bring violence to her door. Eytan's words, that I destroy everything I touch and everyone that gets close to me, echoed in my head. I thought about Mara, who seemed to want nothing from me other than my company, and that if I truly was cursed then perhaps the best thing I could do was leave right now and let Mara forget I ever existed.

She ruffled the towel over my hair and then rested the two ends on my shoulders. We sat and talked, my unease subsiding with every sentence from her lips. I decided to stay and not tell her about what had happened. Enough time had passed that I was sure I hadn't been followed, so in conversation I brushed off the intensity of the phone call as just a run of the mill panic attack and not one spurred by any real danger. I didn't want to worry her, what had happened could wait until the morning, until I spoke to the police. I'd deal with the trauma of what had happened tomorrow, and give myself time to process it all. For now, all I wanted to do was forget the entire thing and enjoy my time with Mara.

After I'd calmed and we were talking easily, Mara began to form a strange smile that increased in size until she could contain it no more, and burst out laughing. I noticed myself in the blackened reflection of the dormant TV screen; the towel dry from Mara had caused my hair to stick up with static and I looked like a Japanese anime character. She giggled and wriggled her nose in the way she did and played with the blue stone around her neck. She raised her hand towards my hair but before she could attempt to neaten it, I leaned in and kissed her.

At first the kiss merely hung upon our lips, a lingering in a timeless moment. I was still expecting her to pull away, but she allowed my lips to rest on hers. After a short while I moved closer, taking her in my arms and moving from a meeting of lips to the passionate kiss of honeymoon lovers. Barely separating our mouths, we motioned to the small wooden ladder. We didn't say a word to each other, as our hips said it all. I backed into the ladder with a thud and Mara pulled away and giggled again. She pulled her shirt over her head and dropped it onto the floor in one fluid motion. She wasn't wearing a bra, and as she unbuttoned her pants and wriggled out of them, her breasts jiggled slightly, the blue stone around her neck swaying with her movements. I followed her example, first removing my shirt and then my jeans. We were both stood in only our underwear, Mara inspecting my body by running the back of her hand up my abdomen to my chest.

She climbed up the ladder and I followed. We continued to kiss as our hands explored each other, before we both removed our last shred of clothing. I grabbed Mara by her calves and pulled her hips towards mine. We continued to kiss as we fucked, Mara ran her hand through my hair and gave it a single tug, hard enough to cause my head to pull back but soft enough to show she was being playful, before giggling and wriggling her nose. My hands were around her hips, but I worked them slowly up her body, past her breasts, wrapping them around her throat. I gave a gentle squeeze and she let out a moan of arousal. I kept my hands around her throat, losing myself more in the moment. I tried hard to not think about Emma, to not allow her memory to taint my want for Mara. I thought about how people said things for comfort, like "this is what she would have wanted." Surely they couldn't really think that. That the only woman I'd ever loved would want me here, in bed with another woman that for all the infatuation, I didn't really know, my hands around her throat as I fucked her without protection. "This is what she would have wanted." No, I doubt that very much.

I felt the push of Mara's hands against my chest, my mind miles away from our embrace. She was trying to push me off her. I was choking her, harder than I intended, not even realising the intensity of my force. Mara coughed and spluttered, her face turning blue.

"Cheldon, please. Stop."

I realised where I was and what I was doing as she choked those three words out. I released my grip and fell backwards towards the foot of her futon. She shuffled herself up towards the head, as far away from me as possible, a look of complete terror in her eyes.

I opened my mouth to apologise, but nothing but empty air tumbled out. She ran her hand along her neck, I could see the deep red markings my grip had left. Mara didn't take her eyes off me; I didn't take mine off her.

"Mara, I didn't…"

My sentence trailed off into nothingness. Unsure if there was ever an intention to finish it, I decided there was only one statement that remained.

"I'll leave."

I began to get up, and as I placed my first foot on the ladder leading down to the floor, I felt Mara's hand on my shoulder.

"No, Cheldon. It's okay. I still want you to stay."

X XXX XXXXXXXX

My awareness sparks into life like flickering
embers rekindling into a new fire, absorbing the
oxygen around and illuminating everything that was
previously darkness. My toes curl around the edge
of the soft dirt under my feet, feeling the lap of the
tranquil water before me. I recognise this body of
water now; I am familiar with this lake. There is a
dark shadow rising to the surface. I want to run but
my feet feel ingrained into the earth. The water
bubbles and boils, a thick white froth foaming on
the surface, and I feel a horrible sinking in my
stomach. A deafening crash booms around and
water shoots up into the air like a tsunami. I can
finally see what has been lying dormant. The long
slender body of a giant serpent emerges and twists
through the atmosphere. It turns its head towards

me, huge teeth contained within a mouth dripping with thick salvia. Its headlight-bright, yellow eyes stare directly into my soul. I try to move but I'm paralysed by its gaze. The heavy, guttural breathing of the creature booms and my ears ache with the noise. I gather the strength and scream at the beast.

"WHAT DO YOU WANT FROM ME?"

An earth-trembling bellow emanates from the monster, the force of which pelts against my skin with the pain of heavy hail. The beast crashes back into the water, causing a tidal wave to cascade over me. I feel the suffocating sensation of drowning as I am consumed wholly by the flood.

Reality snapped back into place and I was stood over Mara's kitchen sink, a large steak knife in my hands, with the infinity and double cross symbol that seemed to be haunting me carved into my arm. Blood ran down my wrist before dripping into the basin. My head was spinning; I couldn't seem to focus on anything except the wound and the knife. The room began to rotate, spinning faster and faster. I tried to steady myself by closing my eyes and breathing deep. When I opened them again, I was knelt on the bed looking down at Mara's sleeping form. The knife was still in my hand, tilted toward her. Unable to control my movements, my mind screamed in agony as I tried to stop the nightmare panning out in front me. I knew this was my body and that it was my hand holding the knife towards Mara's throat, but I felt as if I was a prisoner inside of myself, trapped by whatever darkness has taken control. I tried to call out to Mara, to warn her, but nothing but a barely audible squeak left my mouth. It was enough to stir her, and she shuffled slightly before rolling onto her side. The quilt moved with her, lowering until her upper body was fully bare. That was when I noticed the mark tattooed below her left shoulder, the same as the mark carved into my arm, the mark that was seemingly inescapable.

I had no idea what it meant, Mara having that tattoo, but it made me tremble with terror. I felt as if I was trapped inside a horror film, like the odds had been stacked against me with the intention of grotesque enjoyment for any who observed the terror I was stumbling through. I gained some control over my functions and pulled myself away from Mara, down the ladder, and leaned against the bookshelf. Most of the books were written in what I assumed was Romanian, most looking incredibly old too. I noticed a thin sheet, slightly larger than the rest of the pages, tucked within one of the books. Drawn to the mystery of this, I pulled the entire tome from the shelf and tried to read the title on the cover.

Sfârșitul Timpului Umanității

Unable to decipher a single word of the text I merely took the larger sheet out. The words SINCA VECHE, FRATTII and the number one thousand, five hundred and eleven were written on one side. I turned the piece of paper over. It was a photo of two people stood in a small chapel-like area inside of a cave. The image had faded but it was still clear enough to make out the faces within the shot. It was Mara and Eytan, stood side by side, smiling. I dropped the photo in shock and the room began to spin again. I tried to reach out and grab the bookshelf, but it was seemingly out of reach. All I could do was close my eyes once more and hope it would stop. A heavy feeling within me started to grow, like a seed flowering. It didn't feel like the budding of some pleasant daffodil though, instead felt like the growth of a parasite, like a tapeworm eating me from the inside. The pain became unbearable; I felt myself falling forwards, then the sharp pain as my face hit the floor.

I was awoken by the cold night air. The ground around me was wet, the rain still pouring hard. I searched around with my left hand, feeling my legs spread out in front of me. I noticed the sensation of my back against a hard wall. My vision gradually came back; the first thing I noticed was the knife still in my right hand, my fist clenched around its handle, with my fingers bloody and sore.

The alley I was sat in was dark, but the streetlight from the road gave enough illumination to get a grasp on my surroundings. I was back in my damp clothes, with no recollection of ever getting dressed. What had happened and how did I end up here? Where was Mara? Had I hurt her? Why was she in that photo with the man that had recently pulled me into his bizarre cultish world? I hoisted myself up using a large red metal bin at my side and tried to walk. My steps were unsteady, but progress was being slowly made. The streets were still barren, devoid of human life, and I meandered through them trying to make some sense of the horrors of this god-awful night.

I made it to the bus stop and checked the times, the first bus of the morning was at five thirty. I checked my phone and sat to down to wait out the twelve minutes before its arrival.

I felt sick to my stomach, but more than just common nausea, I felt as if there was something growing inside of me. A demonic tapeworm that was chewing up my insides and feeding on all that was good within. I still had the knife in my hand, my grip still incredibly tight. I hadn't even noticed I'd taken it with me from the alleyway, let alone that I was gripping it with such force. I placed it on the seat next to me and my hand ached with the relief of tension. I was so distant from reality, so focussed on my inner turmoil, that I didn't even notice the clean-cut man in a suit walk up and place his hand on my shoulder.

"Hello, Sheldon."

I looked up towards Michael and smiled. Despite my suspicions of Michael, I was instantly relieved to see his face looking down at me. Michael took a seat next to me, and I crumpled into his embrace.

"It's okay, Sheldon. There's nothing to fear now."

"There's a whole fucking lot to fear, Michael. A whole lot you wouldn't believe even if I told you."

"No, Sheldon. You see, you may feel like you're past the point of no return but there's humanity in you yet. The light has not yet been extinguished completely."

I looked up at Michael, puzzled.

"Michael, what exactly do you know about what's going on?"

He paused, unsure whether to divulge that information to me. Like a journalist unable to reveal their inside source, he held back.

"I know enough."

I shrugged his arms from around me and stood up, turning to him with anger in my eyes.

"No. That's not good enough. It seems like I'm the only person who doesn't have a clue. You turn up out of nowhere and you already know my name. Then you show up again when I'm a mess and you not only know where and who I've been with, but you seem to know my entire fucking history. Now here you are again, appearing when I'm at my worse, with hugs and pleasantries. Just who the hell are you?"

Michael stood up, his face in incredibly close proximity to mine as he did. His words were still kind, but something had changed in his delivery. His tone was almost, for the first time since we met, hostile.

"My child, please. Sit down and let us talk. There's still hope of redemption for you. There's still..."

"Shut the fuck up! Shut up! I'm sick of it! I'm sick of you and your constant chirpy salvation shit babble! I want to know just what the hell you're doing, always on my back. Who are you, Michael? Who are you? Tell me who you are, or I swear to…"

"Sheldon. I've been beyond patient with you and your petulant refusal to accept my help. I promised you a path to salvation, yet you shunned and mocked it. I warned you away from that whore, yet still you persisted. If you don't accept my help now, if you continue on this journey towards the abyss, then things will never get better for you. This unforgiving cycle will continue for eternity, with you trapped in the middle. I didn't know such stubbornness could be genetic. I warned your mother when she decided to tread down the path to her demise, but she was just as stupid as…"

I pushed Michael back and he fell onto the seat. I picked the knife up from the bus-stop seat and plunged it into his stomach. His eyes bulged slightly as the blade went in. I whispered into his ear,

"You cannot change the flow of fate."

I twisted the blade and a small gasp of pain emanated from his mouth. He looked at me and then down towards the knife, his face a picture of disbelief. I pulled the knife out and walked to the curb, dropping it down a grid.

Michael was bleeding and losing consciousness. I took my jacket off and covered his torso with it like a blanket, hiding the dark blood staining his shirt. He passed out, eyes closed, and looked more like a sleeping drunk than a man on the brink of death. After the ire faded, I realised what I had done and began to sob. Why was I so unable to control this rage, this beast deep within me? Just one passing comment about my mother from his lips had flicked a switch and the monster had taken over. It was as if I had two souls within me, my own and that of this dark anger. Perhaps that's what Eytan meant, that it had always been inside of me. These bouts of anger felt so alien when they happened, as if they were not my own actions but that of someone else, yet they had occurred so frequently throughout my life that it was impossible to distance myself from them. The frustration, the blind rage, the aggression towards everyone who had ever tried to help me, they were all me. Perhaps another facet of my being, a chaos from deep within, but me nonetheless. It was strange, I should have felt an immense amount of guilt for what I'd done to Michael, but my tears were not for him. His death was shadowed by the overwhelming agony of realising that the pain I'd caused throughout my entire life had been caused by me, and only me. Whatever dark ancient evil lay within had not been supplanted. I was not possessed by some external demonic force; the evil was me. My mind had simply detached itself from the horror of my anger, to make me feel these actions were not my own, to protect me from the truth. I had created a fantasy where I was without accountability, immune from guilt. The parts of my history that had seemed blurry, sometimes completely empty, were simply stored in some dark recess of my brain to be forgotten as unforgivable sin. Michael had opened the door to all this darkness that had been hiding within me and now he was dead. All he'd wanted to do was help me, to save me from what I now realised to be true.

I was not possessed by a monster; I was the monster.

I left Michael slumped at the bus stop and got the first bus of the morning to return home. Without removing my wet clothes, I paced the small flat above the sandwich shop that I had occupied since leaving the hospital, trying to grab hold of something of metaphysical stability to stop me from falling completely into the chaos. I thought about the photo of Mara and Eytan, and how the two of them could be connected. I couldn't shake the feeling that Mara's story about her life in Romania and Eytan's unbelievable tale of ancient beings were one and the same. I'd fallen for Mara, and I'd like to think she had fallen for me. That perhaps her original intention had been the same as Eytan's, but she had found a connection with me. I wanted to be more to her than just some part of a sinister plot. She'd asked me to stay after I'd hurt her, so perhaps she really did care for me.

I began to attempt to put all these things together, but pieces were still missing. There was still something in me that wanted to hold onto the notion that maybe the whole thing was fictitious. That maybe my refusal to medicate after Emma's death was to blame, or that I had merely found myself trapped by the same brainwashing techniques that so many cults use to ensnare their victims. But even if that were true, it was impossible for me to just let go and return to normality. Whatever the truth was, Michael was dead. I had killed him, and a long stretch in prison or a mental asylum was not something I felt I could survive. No, whatever the reality, I had to continue down this rabbit hole and see this until fruition. I knew what I had to do; it was the only way for me to achieve the redemption Michael had promised. I couldn't kill the beast inside, and I doubted I could get it out of me, but perhaps I could keep it within; take myself and whatever evil was eating me alive far away and stop it from bringing an unholy Armageddon unto the world. This world that had once contained Emma. But Emma was gone, so did I even want to stop it? What kind of world was there to save if the only woman I truly loved was gone? I could never get my happily ever after so why should anyone else? Perhaps I should let go and have this darkness take control.

I shook my head, trying to expel those thoughts. It was hard to determine what were my thoughts and which were those of the beast, and if there was even any difference between the two. Everything I had witnessed over the past few days, things perceivably rooted within reality and others that had come to me in memories, had forced me to greatly question my own sanity. I was not beyond the point of thinking that perhaps the cataclysmic events that were seemingly unfolding around me, were in fact the cause of the decline of my mind into madness. Still, I'd once heard that if you think you're insane then you're most likely not, that losing your mind also means losing your ability to question your mental state. The insane believe themselves to be sane, and my rational doubting and questioning of these events meant that whatever was happening was very likely to be the truth. In many ways this was more terrifying than madness, that the incomprehensible events of the last two weeks of my entire life were a very real fate with a flow I could do nothing to stop.

I headed out the door of my flat, got into the car that had been lying lifeless since the day it arrived, and turned the key in the ignition without fear. The car struggled at first, but eventually the engine growled into life. The anxieties of the past had dissipated. I wondered if I was simply overwrought with a nihilistic streak, focussed more on my goal of self-destruction than the fears that came from the delicacies of my history, or if I was merely losing more of myself to the beast. I thought about the note my father had left for me, the ominous poetry that were his words. "In the Creswell Crags, where the Devil cannot pass" repeated over and over in my brain. My mind filled with this incredible force urging me towards a system of ancient caves I was quite certain I had never before visited. I was sure I'd never been there, but I drove without any prior plan of direction, my body on autopilot, my mind never second guessing any turn. I was drawn towards the location, guided by an invisible beacon, driving the roads with the familiarity of a daily commute. There were a few cars, the early risers, but the drive was mostly one of solitude. The storm that had begun to rage the night before showed no signs of calming, instead getting heavier with each mile closer. I drove in silence, tears running down my face. I couldn't stop the flow of fate, that's what Eytan had said. He'd told me that I was only half full, that only my mother's genes had been passed to me, and I realised in those moments as I drove through the tempest who my father was.

I thought about my mother. I had nothing physical to remember her by, nothing I could hold in my hands, but what traits had I inherited from the woman who brought me into this world? It seemed strange to think that perhaps some of the most integral parts of what made me who I am were coded into my D.N.A., born from a woman I had never met. I had only ever seen photos, but somewhere deep inside me I felt as if I knew her. That if I tried hard enough, I could play out scenes of her life within my own mind like I'd been there myself. I missed her so much, nearly as much as I missed Emma, and we'd never spoken a word. I wanted to know so much about my mother; to love her and have her love me. Eytan had said I was only half full, but in truth I didn't even feel as if I was that.

I arrived at Creswell Crags and pulled over, killing the engine. A giant storm cloud had formed over the system of caves and I saw the form of a great serpent twisting within the tempest, the way the beast had in my dream. As I saw that horrible creature above me, its name echoed loud and clear throughout my mind. I exhaled heavily before taking in a short breath, enough air to utter its name.

"Leviathan."

The radio suddenly came to life, but the key was no longer in the ignition. A familiar riff began to play, and hearing it caused my silent tears to turn into audible sobs. I knew where the river of fate would take me, I knew what this had all been leading me to. If I could, I'd go back to the day Emma died and have never taken my eyes off the goddamn road, never have treated her the way I did. But I couldn't stop the flow of fate, and I knew where I had to go. I'd return to when we met and refuse her number so she wouldn't be dragged into the calamity that was my life, so she'd be somewhere else with anybody else that day I killed her. Michael had called Emma an angel, and because I couldn't keep my demons away, she was now dead. It was my fault. Eytan had called me the boy who destroyed everything he touched; in that he was right. There was so much death that had come simply from my existence; my mother, my uncle, Emma, Michael. I wanted to remedy it all, but I knew I couldn't. All I could do was drift like flotsam on the river of whatever the hell lay before me. There was darkness inside of me, but there was still light. Michael had said so, but I didn't feel that was the case. I was unsure what would happen when I stepped out of the car and headed into the crags, and I had no idea what happened to my father after he left the day I ended up in the hospital, but I would find out soon enough.

I thought about Mara, and though I was sure it was true, I couldn't believe that she and that cult were somehow linked. She had seemed so innocent, like she genuinely cared, but I knew now I was a fool to have let my guard down. I couldn't stop the flow of fate, but I could let it take me. I could give up all resistance and let the waters consume me. I had nothing left, whatever love had been gifted to me throughout my life had either died or betrayed me. If I couldn't stop the flow of fate, if everything that had happened had always been destined to happen, then why bother to fight against it? If every action is predetermined and we're truly unable to move in any direction other than the one already carved out for us, why not just let destiny take its course? When Emma was still alive, she'd speak a lot about how the concept of free will was fiction. I hated the idea of that, not being in control of my fate, and I disagreed vehemently with her. Surely it was obvious that every decision was one that was made by the individual, not by any external force, but she disagreed. She argued that every single event that occurred within a person's life was influenced on a deep unconscious level. That when we believe we are making these decisions of free will, what's truly happening is merely a mathematical outcome, nothing more than the sum of all the parts of our own personal equation. Perhaps our existence wasn't predetermined in the usual understanding, not written in scriptures or decided by some benevolent deity aeons before the decision itself, but still not truly within our own hands. Perhaps we are all nothing but flotsam pulled by the flow of the water, unaware of what's around the river's bend but completely powerless to change course before fate dumps us out into the ocean. I whisper the words as I write them into my notebook,

"So here I sit, outside the door to the endless truth of instability and futility. Pulled by the flow of the water, completely powerless to change course, but with no ocean for me waiting around the river bend. Now I know who I am, where I came from, and what I will become."

The last "ring of fire" sung by Johnny Cash repeated over and over again. I gave a short sharp blast on the dashboard with my clenched fist.

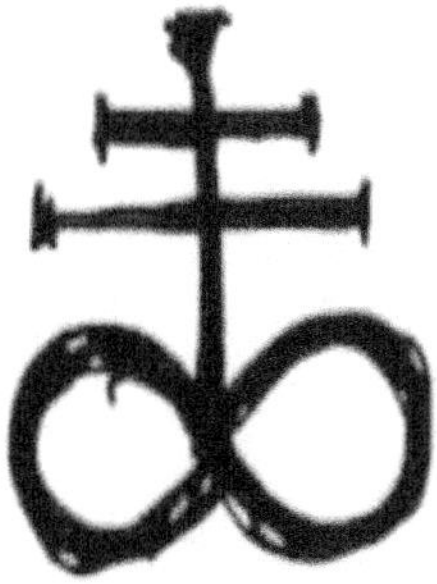

There are a few things I've already discovered since finding this notebook and starting my research. To save anyone who would like to pick up the thread, I'll tell you what I've found.

The bands Ten Foot Wizard and Bong Cauldron are real. I've contacted them both and they've told me that they have no idea about the contents of the notebook. Ten Foot Wizard have assured me that they've never had anyone named Sheldon Belmond work for them, and if this person even exists, they are unaware of ever having met him. I could not find any information about a black metal band from Romania named Crimsona. Louder Than War is an online alternative music magazine, but according to the email correspondence between myself and their Editor in Chief, they do not have, nor ever had, a writer called Simon Belmond.

The John Rylands in Manchester did once have an exhibition named Magic, Witches & Devils in the Early Modern World, and the library does house a segment of what is claimed to be the oldest surviving edition of the Christian Bible. I can find no record of a mental health facility called Junction Thirteen, let alone one with an in-patient facility named Unit Eight.

The Rebellion bar in Manchester is real. The owner's name isn't Eytan, and he does not seem to have any connection with Romania or the occult in any way, from what he has told me. I was kindly given a tour of the venue, and while it does roughly match what was said in the notebook, there was no sign of any sort of "ritual room." I was informed that the venue once had an events manager named Eytan, again with no connection to Romania or the occult, who had unfortunately passed away. As a sign of respect, I dedicate this book to him.

When my girlfriend and I discovered the notebook, we'd been visiting Creswell Crags to see the "witch markings" as part of one of the tours available to the public. After a brief introductory speech, we were taken into one of the many caves and shown the series of strange etchings on the walls inside. The tour guide explained that these were markings that had been used throughout history to keep evil energy away. The one that occurred the most throughout was a VV, often mistaken for a W, which meant "virgin of virgins" symbolising the purity of the Virgin Mary. We were told that although these markings are usually placed to keep evil out, in this instance they believed that they had been placed to keep something evil within. The most curious part of the whole structure, or at least the small segment we were shown, was a large domed area that is believed to have been naturally formed by underground water over centuries. This domed area was filled with these markings, and above a small entrance that led deeper into the cave system but was sealed off from the public, there was a giant VV carved above it. This was not only much larger and etched far deeper into the rock, but it was also upside down, looking like a giant M. I asked what this inverted version could mean, and the guide said they weren't sure. Their theory was that, like the usual VV, this M was symbolic of the Virgin Mary. Though that's entirely possible, and probably the most logical option, after reading that notebook I can't help but think that perhaps that this giant M is referring to someone else.

With the exception of the Creswell carvings and the John Ryland exhibition, which don't actually prove anything relating to the notebook, the above factors all point to the notion that the story told here is one of fiction. I would have agreed and not given these scribblings another thought under *normal circumstances, but since finding the notebook something has been happening that has made me think that perhaps there is something to it all after all. A few days after we visited Creswell Crags, I noticed that I seemed to be being followed by people dressed in black. This has been happening on a pretty regular basis. Though not in robes, they are dressed in black jackets with the hoods up to hide their faces. These people only follow me in busy places, and only when I'm alone. If I try to confront them, they disappear into the crowd and vanish from sight. Perhaps I'm being paranoid, but I'm scared. This is the main reason I want to put this information into the public. Not just in case something happens to me, but in the hope that by doing so I'm left alone. That perhaps someone will unravel more than I have, and the focus will be taken away from me. This is selfish, I know, but I'm constantly checking over my shoulder and it's having such a negative impact on my life that I'm finding difficulty coping. My days are now filled with an awful feeling of impending doom, but this thing has got under my skin, I've been pulled into its orbit and I can't just let it go completely.*

With that in mind, I urge anyone who does decide to delve into this to do so with caution.

If you have any thoughts or information, then
please get in touch on Twitter using @sunbather138

Printed in Great Britain
by Amazon

59740130R00132